Frankenswinger

To Linda & Bud,

You guys rule!

Love, Nick

NICK BAKER

outskirtspress

DENVER, COLORADO

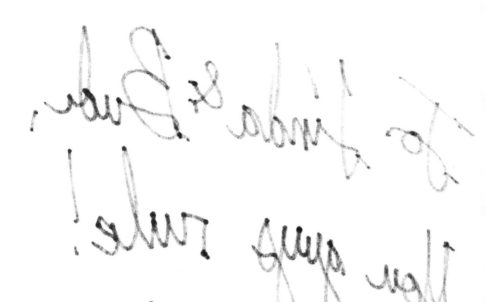

Outskirts Press, Inc.
http://www.outskirtspress.com

ISBN: 978-1-4327-9374-6

Outskirts Press and the "OP" logo are trademarks belonging to Outskirts Press, Inc.

PRINTED IN THE UNITED STATES OF AMERICA

To Bob Baker & Bob Wilson

Chapter One

"This can't be possible."

"Just look again", Vince insisted.

Jerry rubbed his eyes and peered back down to his microscope and onto the Petri dish below him. After he refocused the lenses, he concentrated intensely and tried not to blink.

"This is the third time. This can't be just an accident," Vince said. He was beside himself with astonishment. "The first batch, the second, … Both dead. Now this one and it's the same. These cultures are alive now. We have to tell Jacobs. We-"

"No, wait," Jerry stopped him. He raised his hand, but kept his eyes fixed on the microscope. "Slow down. Just wait. We don't know what we're looking at yet and we're not going to let that stuck up dork take the credit for this. Now let's go over this one more time."

Jerry stood up and both of them paced around the laboratory, stared into space, and tried to think. Vince glanced over his clipboard. Jerry could hear him when his back was turned, as he flipped pages and muttered to himself. Then there was silence except for the low humming of the laboratory's fluorescent lights and Jerry turned to face him again. Vince wandered the room while he slowly pantomimed the actions from his memory and checked the label on the side of the sample's dish.

"The SW mixture and we were up to which series? It was series V, Ummm… Version 3. Let's go over it again. We know the samples failed because I set the fridge temperature five degrees too warm. You didn't notice until after you started to examine them. The V3 sample was alive and growing while all the others were toast." Vince stood still and his eyes met Jerry's.

"Have you ever seen or even heard of something like this before? Anything close?" Jerry asked. Vince just stared at him. They shared an uncomfortable silence until Vince slowly shook his head.

"This is magic, not science," Vince huffed. "Until somebody figures out how this is working."

"Not somebody, man. Us," Jerry smiled. He approached Vince, patted him on the shoulder and led him towards to exit. He took a tall, sealed bottle labeled "MR-SW-V3," jiggled it playfully, and put it in his lab coat pocket as they walked out. "We've got a lot to think about here. Let's take a coffee break and talk this over."

The hallways of Mansell Labs were empty. It was almost midnight that Friday and most of the massive complex's employees had left early to enjoy the weekend. Jerry and Vince could hear their voices echo down the cavernous, sterile, white hallways even though they spoke just above a whisper.

"These neurons remain regenerated at room temperature, not just five degrees warmer," Vince said. "We've done it. But how? This could not be what Jacobs was looking for. This was an accident."

"And done by nobodies like us," Jerry chuckled. "This thing is so secret and so spread out through all the other labs that no one even knows what we're looking for. No one will ever find out."

They walked into the building's cafeteria to find it was also empty, but there was still a half a pot of coffee still left out. Jerry poured two small styrofoam cups full and handed one to Vince. When they pulled out a couple of plastic chairs from under one of the tables, the chair's feet made an annoying metal screech on the linoleum floor. Each of them took sips from their cups as they sat down and grimaced from its temperature and stale, burnt flavor. They sat across from each other at one of the many six-foot rectangular tables and pondered their situation. Vince leaned forward gradually, motioned as if he were to speak, and then backed down. He repeated this two more times before he finally spoke.

"I...I don't know, Jerry. I mean, what do we have our hands on here?" Vince asked timidly. "If these samples are truly regenerated brain tissue and they can stay alive at room temperature, what would this do to say, a whole brain? How would this affect other tissue, living or dead? Oh God, there'll...There'll have to be tests, hundreds... Thousands of them. We're in over our heads here."

Jerry could see that Vince was growing anxious. Cold beads of sweat began to form on his doughy brow, but he couldn't help but feel elated. Vince's eyes darted about while his mind churned like an angry beehive. He tried to steady himself and took a quick puff from his asthma inhaler. Vince focused again on Jerry when he saw a wide grin that stretched across his face.

"Wha...What?" Vince stammered.

"Look," Jerry said. "They don't know what they have here either. Now consider this. You and I could take this thing, quit, and develop V3 on our own. Mansell Labs has no patents. This is just experimental. Jacobs doesn't know anything about this and he certainly doesn't care if we come or go."

"But it's their formula." Vince responded.

"Yes, but they don't know the right proportion of components. Whatever application they intended to use for this formula, it clearly was for living subjects, not dead ones. With all the other combinations, it would take them forever to find this mixture," Jerry replied. "Besides, we could always dilute it or add some inactive ingredient like, say sugar. They'd never know."

"What about the confidentiality agreement?" Vince asked and started to become more agreeable.

"After one year, it won't matter," Jerry replied quickly. "It'll take us nearly that long to set up shop in the first place and these guys would have forgotten all about us by then. Merck, Pfiser, Eli Lily? They'll all be falling over themselves for this."

Vince let out a prolonged exhale and wiped the sweat off his brow with his hand. He tapped his chubby fingers on his other hand on the table for a moment, sipped his coffee, and spoke again, "I dunno, man. It's not the money, really, and you know that I need it more than anybody."

"You keep moaning about your student loans and how you'll never get to retire in luxury on a tropical island. Then this drops in your lap. I mean, what are the odds?" Jerry insisted. "Come on. No one ever gets rich on a salary."

"There could be some dangerous applications for this." Vince said bluntly.

"Yeah, like what?" Jerry chuckled back.

They both were startled by a flash, out the window, and off in the distance. The low rumbling of thunder soon followed it. The rumble slowly echoed and decayed.

"It's that dry lightning stuff again, leftovers from that storm in Baja. Just in time for fire season too. But anyway, hell, I don't know," Vince said. "Look, if this can do what I think we both are thinking it can do… Well…. Suffice to say, it can change the world forever. Can you begin to imagine what could happen if we can bring the dead back to life? If it fell into the wrong hands, it-"

"And what if it fell into the right hands?" Jerry interrupted. "We're talking Nobel Prize winning stuff here! Or would you rather just hand this over to Jacobs? He's not exactly my idea of 'the right hands'." He did an air quotes hand gesture at the end.

Vince bit his lip gently and stewed over it in silence. He shook his head every few seconds. Jerry eventually stood from his chair and threw away his half empty cup of coffee.

"Alright, alright," he motioned to Vince to follow him out. "It's obvious that we're not going to sort this all out tonight. The lab's shut down anyway. I'll take a sample of this mixture home and run a few more tests, then we come back fresh as a daisy on Monday, OK?"

"Yeah, I guess," Vince sighed heavily, chugged the rest of his coffee before he threw out the cup, and followed him out of the cafeteria. "It's always best to sleep on things like this. At least, that's what Poppa always says."

"Wise man," Jerry patted him on the shoulder. "How's he doing these days?"

"Fine, the same," he replied. "Still shut in, watching game shows all day, playing with his toy trains. He really needs to get out more."

"Don't we all."

The security guard was gone from his post at the front door, so they let themselves out. It hadn't been raining, but low, dark clouds blanketed the night sky. Vince walked ahead of Jerry a few feet next to a row of trees, and he started to fidget with his keychain. He finally found the key to his car and held it between his thumb and index finger. As he turned to face Jerry again, the key slipped from his hand and landed on the ground next to one of the trees. Vince held onto the tree for balance, as he leaned over to pick the keychain up, and grunted.

"I doubt I'll get any slee-..."

FLASH!

A thin, crooked bolt of lightning snaked down from the sky and struck the tree. The discharge was strong enough to knock Jerry backwards. He fell on the pavement, howled, and clutched his blinded retinas. His retina burns gradually faded as he stretched out his arms, struggled to catch his breath, and get on his feet again. He could make out Vince's body splayed out on the ground, which reeked from the foul odor of singed hair. The stricken tree, now stained black, fizzled and popped faintly. What few remaining leaves burned into smoldering embers, fell off, and gently drifted into the parking lot. Still dazed, Jerry shambled forward.

"Vince? Vince?" his raspy voice croaked.

Jerry knelt before Vince, placed his hand on his neck and wrist, and checked for a pulse. Seconds passed and he felt nothing. His eyes cleared up enough that he could make out Vince's inert, flabby face and adrenaline began to coarse through his veins.

"Oh God! Oh no! Vince! Vince! Wake up!" Jerry shouted, but to no avail. He put his hand behind Vince's neck, elevated his head, and opened Vince's lifeless jaw with his other hand. The moment he was about to start to resuscitate him, Jerry hesitated and recoiled slightly at the sight of a stream of warm drool draining down the side of Vince's mouth. He steadied himself, shut his eyes for a moment, and mumbled, "OK. He'd do it for me. He'd do it for me."

Jerry took a deep breath, sealed his mouth over Vince's, and filled his lungs with air. He repeated this three times. Vince did not respond, so he began compressions on Vince's chest, and then did another round of breaths, but still to no avail. Panic began to set in and Jerry jumped to his feet again. He yelled back to the lab and his shouts echoed into the silent night, "Help! Help! Anybody!"

He desperately scanned around for another person, but they were indeed alone. Without thinking, he sprinted back into the lab, picked up the phone at the empty desk of the security guard, and frantically dialed 911. It rang twice until a voice answered, "911 Emergency."

"Hello! Hello!" Jerry could barely talk coherently, "Send an ambulance over to the entrance of Mansell Labs immediately! My friend has been struck by lightning! I've tried CPR, but he's still unresponsive! I'm going to try again! Hurry!"

He dropped the receiver on the desk and bolted for the door again. As he ran, he could hear the operator still saying, "We have your location. An ambulance is in route to you now. Hello? Hello?"

Jerry was just about to go outside when he stopped dead in his tracks and reached into his pocket. He felt the vial in there for a moment and then quickly whipped it out. He still had the V3 sample. Cold beads of sweat trickled down his head and his breathing became more and more shallow while he paused to ponder. Jerry jerked a step towards the lab, then stopped, and stepped in the other direction.

After doing this a couple times, he snapped out of it and dashed back into his lab. He snatched the first syringe he could get his hands on and bolted outside again. Jerry pounced on Vince's body and tried CPR one more time, but there was still no change.

He took the needle of the syringe, drew as much of the V3 formula into its chamber until it was full, and desperately tried to calm down, to keep his hands from shaking. He squirted out a little liquid, which freed the chamber from any air bubbles, and felt around Vince's neck for the carotid artery. Jerry still couldn't feel a pulse, but took his best guess and placed the tip of the needle at Vince's neck, pressed delicately, but hesitated to break the skin.

"God help me," he whispered to himself and closed his eyes for a moment. He opened them again, focused as much as he could, and shoved the needle through the skin into Vince's neck. He steadied his hand, injected the entire contents of the chamber, deftly removed it once it was empty, and put it in his coat pocket. Jerry put his ear to Vince's chest and hoped that he would hear a heartbeat, but again nothing. He began to cry, but he was hopeful when he heard the sound of the ambulance's siren in the distance. Jerry leapt to his feet again, jumped up and down, and waved his arms frantically. "Here!" he shouted. "Over here! Hurry!"

The shiny white ambulance with bright green stripes steered towards them. Its sirens blazed until it came to a halt. A pair of EMTs burst out of the back doors with a stretcher and they quickly began to examine Vince.

"Still no pulse?" one of the EMTs asked Jerry.

"No." Jerry shook his head and backed away to give them more room.

The other EMT pried open each of Jerry's eyelids, one at a time, and shined her small flashlight into them.

"No dilation. This one's cold," she said quickly.

"Get him inside!" the EMT shouted to the other. "Charge the defibrillator! Go! Go!"

Jerry helped the two EMTs get Vince's body onto the stretcher and into the ambulance. They were about to shut the ambulance's doors when one of the EMTs motioned to Jerry to back away.

"We need room here!" he ordered him. "Follow us to St. John's on Santa Monica!"

Jerry had just enough time to nod when the doors slammed shut and the ambulance careened out of the parking lot and blared its sirens again. He dashed to his 1984 Toyota Camry, barely got his keys into the ignition with his trembling hands, and stepped hard on the gas.

The moment Jerry made it out of the parking lot, the lab's security guard shuffled back to his post at the front door desk, oblivious to what had happened. He had been listening to classic rock blasted at full volume through his iPod the whole time and was still banging his head to the beat. He chewed on a candy bar that he'd just bought from a vending machine down the hall. The guard finally noticed that the phone receiver was off the hook at his desk, but he simply hung it up, unable to hear on the other end as the 911 operator pleaded, "Hello? Hello? Can you hear me?" He sat down on his rolling chair, took off his shoes, and put his feet up on the desk.

Though the ambulance had pulled a long distance away from Jerry, he eventually caught up as they both negotiated through intersection after intersection. As soon as the hospital came into sight, the ambulance got caught behind a moving van.

"Come on!" Jerry shouted and pounded his fist on the dashboard. The moving van gradually pulled over and the ambulance screeched its tires, as it got moving again. Jerry pulled in, parked just outside the emergency entrance, bolted out, and slammed his car door behind him. He could see the EMTs were carrying in Vince as he ran closer and was horrified to see that they hadn't revived him. He finally caught up with them as they all went inside through sliding glass doors. One of the EMTs turned back and restrained Jerry by his shoulders as the others passed into the emergency room.

"Stay back!" she ordered. "You can't help him."

"Is he dead?!" Jerry demanded. "Tell me! Is he dead!?!"

The EMT looked sternly back at him and admitted, "It's not looking good." She disappeared into the swarm of activity in the emergency room. Jerry exhaled loudly and clenched his hands on top of his head.

He fidgeted in the waiting room for about ten minutes, though but it felt like hours to him. Eventually, a young black woman in surgical scrubs entered the waiting room holding a clipboard.

"Who came in with Vincent Mercurio?" she asked.

"I did!" Jerry stepped forward and his eyes lit up. His expression instantly faded when he saw the woman take off her surgical mask and revealed her exhausted frown.

"I'm Dr. Sawyer," she said flatly. "Can you follow me please?"

Jerry nodded and cringed to himself as he followed her down a hall. He couldn't contain himself any longer and stopped her just before they were about to enter an empty room.

"Please!" he begged. "Just tell me now. Did he survive?"

She shook her head no as they entered and Jerry gasped after she shut the door behind them.

"I'm sorry…" her voice haltered as she hinted that she wanted to know his name.

"Jerry." he blurted.

"Jerry," she continued. "I'm so sorry. We tried everything we could to revive him, but we never regained a pulse. Are you related to him?"

"He's…Uhh…" Jerry almost said he worked with him, but hesitated. "We're old friends."

"Are you in touch with his next of kin?" she asked.

"Yes," he replied sadly, as his eyes lowered down. "His father, I think, is his only relative around here that I know about."

"We can notify him," she offered.

"*No!*" he replied immediately, and then lowered his voice, "I mean, please. He was his only son and... Uhh... He's a widower as well. Please, let me tell him... Tell him in the morning. I...I can't tell him this now. Please?"

Dr. Sawyer nodded solemnly, patted him on the shoulder, and led him out of the room and to the front of the hospital. She turned to him once again as he exited.

"You can tell Mr. Mercurio that his son will be here and we'll be happy to help with any arrangements he makes." She nodded and shook Jerry's hand. "Once again, I'm sorry we couldn't save him."

"No... No..." he said quietly, though unable to look her in the eye, "Thank you for trying".

Jerry shuffled in a daze out into the dark parking lot. He shook his head in disbelief and muttered under his breath to himself. He didn't even notice a convoy of police cars and ambulances as they pulled in behind him, despite how loudly their sirens wailed. After he got inside his car, Jerry rested his forehead on the steering wheel and silently tried to digest all that had just happened.

Outside and oblivious to Jerry, a group of paramedics and policemen brought in two gang members and a policeman, all three wounded from a nearby shootout. Dr. Sawyer had just re-entered the emergency room and began to treat one of the wounded gang members. He was limp and his eyes were closed, severely wounded from a pistol bullet that pierced his chest, and his breathing was becoming shallower.

One of the police officers broke off from the others to guard the second wounded gang member, who'd been shot in the lower abdomen, appeared unconscious, but his breathing was steady. The officer unlocked his set of handcuffs that bound the second gang member's wrist to the gurney and Dr. Sawyer and her nurses quickly moved him across from his gurney to an operating table. As they began to treat him, the police officer re-attached the cuffs to the operating table and backed away to give them more room.

"Flatline!" shouted the doctor who treated the first, more wounded gang member. The startled officer spun around and turned his back to the operating table.

It distracted Dr. Sawyer, the police officer, and the others just long enough, as a surge of adrenaline kicked in on her patient. Playing possum until he could get a chance to escape, his eyes popped open. The second, less wounded gang member reached across the operating table, snatched the officer's pistol from its holster, and shot him point plank in the center in his back. The officer's bulletproof vest stopped the bullet, but the impact made the officer scream in pain and lurch forward. He collided with two nurses and another officer, which knocked them all into a dog pile on the floor.

This gave the gang member just enough time to pop off another round, which severed the handcuff chain, and freed him from the operating table. After he leapt to his feet, he grappled with Dr. Sawyer until he held her tightly from behind with the pistol aimed at the side of her head.

"Get back! Get back! Now!" he barked at everybody. The wounded policeman, the other officer, and the nurses were helped to their feet and took cover behind all the other policemen, who had drawn out their pistols and attempted to get a clear line of fire at the gang member.

"Don't shoot! Do as he says!" Dr. Sawyer pleaded and she allowed the gang member to drag her backwards towards the emergency room exit. The policemen kept their distance and noticed a slow trickle of blood started to run down the gang member's pant leg that left a thin streak stain on the linoleum floor.

Nobody witnessed that on the other side of the emergency room, the index finger on Vince's right hand slowly began to move.

The mob scene in the emergency room continued out into the street as Jerry switched on his car radio, and tried to break out of his state of shock. The radio had been left on the local oldies station earlier that day when he drove to work, and he groaned when he realized the song playing was "Wouldn't It Be Nice" by the Beach Boys. He pulled out of the parking lot, and didn't pay any attention at all what had been going on in his rear view mirror, but he switched off the radio after driving a couple blocks.

Vince's chest rose and fell as he took his first breath. His eyes opened and squinted at first from the bright fluorescent bulbs above him. Vince stood up in his bed and rubbed his temples. He felt the pain of a dull, throbbing headache and began to moan. An overpowering ringing in his ears muffled the shouting from inside and outside the emergency room. He saw that his wallet and eyeglasses were on a table next to him, so he instinctually picked them up, put his wallet in his pants pocket and his eyeglasses on his head. His feet plopped off the bed and onto the floor. Unbalanced at first, he was able to shamble his way out of the emergency room, though he could barely make out the shapes of the other people through his blurred vision, despite having put on his eyeglasses.

He made it past the mob scene outside and started down Santa Monica Boulevard as the gang member who held Dr. Sawyer hostage finally passed out from his blood loss. She slipped out of his grip safely and the surrounding policemen closed in on them. In an instant, one of the officers kicked away the pistol from his limp hand, and another restrained and handcuffed him again.

Vince sniffled a little and tried to clear his sore, groggy throat while he continued down the sidewalk. He could feel his head slowly clear up and the ringing of his ears dissipate as he completed almost a mile of walking. Feeling around in his pants pockets, he eventually noticed that his keychain was missing.

"Oh, that's just great," he finally was able to croak out some words to himself. "Perfect. Where the hell am I? … Maybe I can catch a bus on Sepulveda."

He was relieved to find that there was still a decent amount of cash in his wallet, so he shuffled down the street, and peered into the distance as his eyesight slowly began to focus again. Vince sighed in relief when an unoccupied taxi appeared and he flagged it down. The taxi's passenger side window rolled down and a fat, hairy man was driving.

"Where to, pal?" he asked with a gravelly, Texas accent.

"Uhh…" Vince tried to collect his thoughts. "How much to Culver City?"

The cab driver thought about it for a little, and then replied, "Ah, call it ten. I'm on my way home anyway."

Vince focused his eyes keenly on the cash in his wallet till he was able to make out the number ten in one of the bill's corners. He fished it out, handed it to the cab driver through the window, got slowly into the back seat, and moaned softly as he did so.

"Sounds like you had a hell of night, eh bubba?" the cab driver joked as they sped away. Vince cringed, nodded silently in agreement, closed his eyes, and rubbed his temples again.

A couple miles down the street, the cab passed by a convenience store, where Jerry was parked. Mortified by what had happened that night, Jerry sat in the parking lot and brooded for some time. As he stoically held back his tears, Jerry went inside, and bought a pint of Jack Daniels from the storekeeper. He slumped back into the driver's seat of his car, briefly considered drinking the bottle right there, unscrewed its cap, but then reconsidered, and screwed it back on again.

"I'll drink it there…. Before I go in." Jerry said quietly to himself. He put the bottle under his seat, started the ignition, and continued down the street towards Culver City.

After Vince's cab made it to his dad's house, he thanked the cab driver and gave him a couple extra dollars tip. Before he shuffled up to the front door, the motion sensor above the porch clicked on a bright security light that blinded Vince for a moment. He held his hand up, shielded his eyes, and moaned again. Having remembered once more that he was missing his keys, he went around the corner of the house and found the spare front door key under a hide-a-way rock in his father's flowerbed. Vince unlocked the front door, went inside the dark house, and the door shut behind him.

The porch's security light clicked off just as Jerry's car pulled in and parked across the street. Jerry sighed heavily and shook his head, as he pulled out the whiskey bottle from under the drivers seat, unscrewed the top, and took a long belt from it. He gasped and growled to himself after he swallowed. The lukewarm whiskey burned his throat.

"Vince," he whimpered as tears began to stream down his cheeks. "Damn, man…"

Chapter Two

"On top of everything that's happened tonight, you say your hospital is missing a different patient's body?" Kate Lippold's asked and her interest piqued.

"Yeah, strange, huh?" Dr. Sawyer replied. She reclined back in her chair and took a sip of water from a paper cup. "Though I wouldn't make much of it. In all the confusion, he probably got mixed up down at the morgue, sent to another hospital, or something. Damned if I know. I've been a little distracted tonight."

"Oh, believe me. I understand," Kate smiled. She rose from her chair and shook Dr. Sawyer's hand. "Thank you so much for your time here tonight. I know it's late."

"That's OK," she answered, "Besides, I'm still way too shook up to sleep tonight."

Before Kate could make it out of the open door behind her, Jim Perez, her cameraman, turned a corner and nearly collided with her as he tried to enter. They backed away from each other and then he stood aside to allow her to pass.

"Jeez, are we done now?" Jim asked, impatient as always.

"No, one more thing," she answered. He growled and followed her outside to their news van. "I want to try to track down this 'lightning' kid."

"Oh, man," Jim's growling grew louder as he loaded his camera gear into the van. "Kate, it's passed midnight! Have you even read the new contract? I'm in golden time here, you know. You know Fulmer's never going to approve this. Nobody even knows where this kid is."

"We know they picked him up at Mansell Labs up the street," she retorted quickly. "At this time of night, his car's probably the only one left there. We make a run on its plates and presto. Problem solved. C'mon, Jim. When's the last time somebody got struck by lightning down here?"

"Whatever." he mumbled and closed the van's sliding side door.

The sound of heavy bass thumping from hip-hop music from the stereo of a passing car was just enough to wake Jerry. His crusty eyelids creaked open and he reeled from the bright sunrise as he lifted his head off the steering wheel, which left a crimson red indention on his forehead. Jerry whined in agony and weakly tried to clear his throat, as his eyes focused. The tell tale empty whiskey bottle was still between his thighs and the sight of it made him want to wretch. He opened the car door and gathered just enough strength to stand. After he stumbled past the curb, Jerry straightened up and gently placed the whiskey bottle by the gutter.

He took a deep breath, closed his eyes, and then let out a prolonged yawn. When he opened his eyes again, the sight of Vince's house in front of him flooded his mind once more with the memory of what had happened the night before and the terrible news that he would have to bring to Vince's father. Jerry choked up his tears, took another deep breath, and then mustered the courage to stagger forward until he was standing right at the front door. He hesitated for a few seconds as the gravity of the situation slowly sank in, but he rang the doorbell subconsciously. Jerry felt increasingly light headed as he heard the muffled footsteps behind the door grow louder. Mr. Mercurio opened it.

"Good lord, Jerry. You look terrible," Mr. Mercurio said with his thick New York accent. He lowered his reading glasses off his nose a little and winced at the sight of Jerry's disheveled appearance. "What happened to you?"

"Mr. Mercurio?" Jerry focused on breathing deeply and tried his best not to faint. "Umm, can I come in?"

"Yeah, sure." he answered nonchalantly.

"I think you might want to sit down." Jerry said with a trembling voice.

"Yeah, right," Mr. Mercurio laughed. "Looks like you're the one who needs to sit."

Jerry followed him into the kitchen.

"Hey Jerry," Vince muttered and sat at the kitchen table with a mouth full of Cheerios.

"Hey Vince," Jerry replied instinctually. Then, like a bucket of ice water hit him, Jerry screamed and fell over backwards onto the kitchen floor. "*AHHHH!!!*"

Vince and his father immediately recoiled from his outburst. Vince nearly choked on his mouthful of cereal, but managed to swallow it. Within seconds, Jerry turned a shade of sickly white and his eyes rolled back in his skull and a wave of uncontrollable nausea swept over him. Though stunned, Vince took a step towards Jerry, just as Jerry clasped his hand over his mouth, let out a muffled retch, and then he bolted for the nearest bathroom.

"Oh, dear God!" Mr. Mercurio bellowed. He followed Vince to the open bathroom door and they were horrified to witness Jerry violently dry heave over the toilet bowl. The very sounds of him retching made them squeamish. "That's disgusting! What awful thing did he drag you to this time, huh?" he accused Vince.

"Who me?" Vince responded.

"Yeah, you!" he shot back.

Jerry curled up his shivering body on the tiled floor, wiped away a thin stream of spit from his mouth, clutched his knotted abdomen, and deliriously attempted to breathe and stay conscious. When his eyes focused again on Vince, panic surged through him once more.

"*AHHH!!!*" Jerry's second scream was even louder. "*AHHHH!!!!!!!!*"

"Whoa!" Vince put up his hands and tried to edge closer to Jerry, but he cringed away deeper into the bathroom's corner. "What the hell is the matter with you?"

"I can't believe this!" Mr. Mercurio paced up and down his hallway fuming with frustration. "You two are scientists! You of all people should be the last ones to get all hopped up like this! I suppose you've been doing this every Friday night, huh?"

"What? No!" Vince turned back to his father. "Friday? Today's Friday! Last night was Thursday."

Jerry peeked up from his fetal position upon hearing that.

"Oh, you must be really into some heavy stuff, pill-head!" he got even angrier. "My son, the pill-head! It's Saturday! Last night was Friday!"

"No, it wasn't!" Vince insisted and then turned back to Jerry. "Jerry, come on, man. You've got to pull yourself together! We've got to be at the lab in an hour. Ah, forget it. You're better off just calling in sick. Jacobs would freak out if he saw you like this."

"It's Saturday!" Mr. Mercurio barked. He marched back into his kitchen, picked up the newspaper off the counter, unfolded it, and shoved it in Vince's face. "*SA-TUR-DAY!*"

Vince took the paper and squinted at the masthead. Jerry gained enough composure to stagger to his feet, but looked around dizzily, still in a state of shock. Vince bit his lower lip slightly, motioned as if to speak, hesitated, and then he studied the paper again. Mr. Mercurio finally got fed up and snatched the paper back from him.

"Still can't remember, huh?" Mr. Mercurio sneered. His focus instantly snapped upstairs. "My God! I bet you've been in my Ambien!"

"Aw, Dad." Vince snickered as his father's absurdity distracted him from the confusion. Undeterred, Mr. Mercurio marched upstairs to the upstairs bathroom and opened its medicine cabinet.

"I heard on the TV that you kids get goofy on these things if you stay awake! I'm counting them, boy! I've only taken three so far from this bottle and if even ones missing, you're in deep trouble, mister!"

Vince could hear his dad's voice from upstairs. Vince folded his arms and stared at Jerry.

"OK, Jerry. Start talking!" he stepped up to him.

"Uhh...I...You..." Jerry stammered.

"15...16...17," they could hear Mr. Mercurio while he counted to himself upstairs.

"You...You..." Jerry continued trying to make sense of all this. "You don't remember anything from last night?"

"Last night?" Vince was baffled. "We finished the U series at the lab and were going to start the V's fresh in the morning. I had some hot cocoa and hit the hay. That was Thursday. Where the hell did we go last night?"

"So, you don't remember Friday at all?" Jerry asked.

"No," he replied.

"Are you sure? Nothing?" Jerry pressed on.

"No!" Vince shook his head. Jerry paced about a moment, stopped, shut his eyes, and slapped himself as hard as he could. "Jerry! God! Stop it! Look at me!"

"OK," Jerry took a deep breath and opened his eyes. He could hear Mr. Mercurio while he marched back downstairs, so he tried to sound as convincing as possible. Mr. Mercurio stood in front of them with his arms folded and narrowed his eyes. "OK. OK. Maybe we did go to some party last night. Yeah..."

"Well?" Vince asked his dad.

"So you haven't been popping my Ambien, fine," he admitted.

The three stared at each other quietly for a moment, unable to grasp the situation. Jerry was about to speak to break the uncomfortable silence when the doorbell rang. The shock caused him to flinch so hard that it hurt his neck. As Jerry winced and massaged his neck, while Vince went to answer the door. Distracted, Jerry pantomimed with his hands to him not to open it, but Vince simply rolled his eyes and ignored his pleas. He swung the door open to behold the beautiful

Kate Lippold on his porch with Jim the cameraman. For a moment, time stood still for Vince.

"Kate Lippold, Eyewitness News." she extended her hand for him to shake, but she was abruptly cut off as Mr. Mercurio slammed the door closed. Startled by his dad's reaction, Vince backed away from him a step. Outside, Kate and Jim looked at each other with mild bewilderment.

"What the hell did you do that for?" Vince whispered loudly.

"I knew it! I knew you idiots have been up to no good!" he shouted and came between Vince and the door. "Get that lady out of here! Now! I don't want any pictures! None, do you understand? I'll smash that goddamn camera! I swear to God!"

"Dad! Stop it. Now you're the one who sounds like he's on drugs," Vince went around his father and opened the door again and spoke to Kate. "Sorry about that. My dad always had a phobia of cameras."

"That thing had better not be turned on, buster, or I'll sue!" Mr. Mercurio said from behind Vince. He covered up his face with one hand and pointed accusingly at Jim with the other. Kate nodded to Jim, who reluctantly put his camera on the floor of the porch and backed away.

"No, no, no," Kate tried to reassure them. "Nothing's rolling. I just have a couple of questions. Is this the home of Vincent Mercurio?"

"Yeah, I…" Vince stopped, noticed that Kate was holding his keychain, smiled, and pointed at them. "Hey, my keys! How did you get those?"

"Uhh…" Kate instinctually handed the keys to Vince and was uncharacteristically at a loss for words. "Wait a minute. You…. Err…."

Before Vince could answer her, Jerry grabbed Vince and pulled him back into the house. Jerry smiled nervously at Kate, "Uhh, just a moment, please."

Jerry slammed the door shut in her face once more. She looked at Jim again, this time in shock and amazement. "Call this in, now!

We might have to go live!" she whispered to Jim, who spun around, walked out to the lawn with his cell phone, and began to dial. Kate put her ear to the front door and tried to hear what was being said on the other side, but could only hear muffled whispers.

"What are you doing?" Vince asked Jerry, who joined his father to block him from the front door. "You guys are acting crazy."

"Vince, wait!" Jerry pleaded as he tried to cut him off from opening the door again. Vince had clearly become agitated and he shoved both of them out of the way. Jerry tried to stop him again as he reached for the doorknob, but Vince edged him away forcefully with his shoulder. Jerry recovered and then tried to advance again, but it was too late. Kate had just enough time to recoil her ear away from the door and smile as Vince swung the door open one more time.

"Sorry about that." Vince apologized.

"Oh, that's alright," she giggled nervously. "No problem, really. So… Uhh… You are Vincent Mercurio?"

"Vince, please," he replied. "Yeah, that's me. Thanks for finding my keys. Where did you find them?"

"Umm. Can I come inside?" she asked timidly.

Vince looked back at his father and Jerry hiding on the other side of the partially opened door. They both waved their hands around and silently mouthed, "No!" in desperation. His annoyance continued to mount until Vince sighed heavily, scratched his head a little, and faced Kate again.

"Look, umm…Kate?" he asked, "I've got a couple things to straighten out here before I can talk to you. Do you mind waiting outside here for a bit? I promise it won't be for very long."

"Oh, fine," she replied immediately, smiled, and tried to contain her excitement. "Take your time. I'll be right here."

Vince shut the door, pointed his index finger forcefully at Jerry, then his father, and silently beckoned them to return to the kitchen. They followed him and he fumed with anger as he turned to Jerry.

"OK, Jerry," he demanded, "Spill it, now! What's going on here?"

Having realized that he couldn't stall any longer, Jerry took a deep breath and gathered his thoughts.

"Look, Vince," he began his confession. "I think you'd better sit down, both of you."

"Oh hell, here it comes." Mr. Mercurio groaned as he and his son sat at the kitchen table. They waited a moment anticipating as Jerry hemmed and hawed to himself.

"Ugh. OK, there's no easy way to say this, so I'll just have out with it," Jerry mumbled quickly. "You died last night, Vince. You were struck by lightning."

Vince and his father were speechless. They looked at each other and Mr. Mercurio's eyes slowly began to well up with tears. He tried to hold back a tidal wave of emotion. He put one hand over his mouth, breathed deeply, simply leaned over from across his chair, gently embraced Vince's shoulder with his other, and rubbed it for a second before he leaned back again.

"Dead?" Vince asked.

"As a doornail. I tried reviving you. It didn't work," he continued. "The paramedics came and took you to the hospital and they couldn't revive you either. I was told you were dead, but I didn't want to wake your father in the middle of the night with this news, so I waited till this morning."

"How? Uhh…How long was I?…" Vince stammered out the words.

"Oh! Uhh…" Jerry rubbed his eyes and worked to clear the cobwebs from his head. "I…Uhh… From the time you were hit to the time you were pronounced dead? God…Ummm…About twenty-five minutes? Over twenty minutes at least."

"How did he get here?" Mr. Mercurio finally spoke up.

"I don't know," Jerry shook his head, then looked at Vince, and asked, "Do you?"

"No…. No," Vince tried to jog his memory, but it was no good.

His father looked at him with a puzzled expression, but Vince insisted. "Really! I thought it was Friday. I woke up in my bed like any other day. I can't remember a thing."

"Great," Mr. Mercurio regained his composure from his grief, but began to grow nervous. "We… We've got to get you back to the hospital! There still might be something wrong with you!"

"No!" Vince shot back instantly, but then cooled down. "No. I feel fine and I'm not going to let those vultures stick me with the add-ons. Oh, Jesus. Our health plan had better cover that ambulance ride. I have a mind to sue them for losing me in the first place!"

"Don't!" his father blurted as his nervousness turned into a wave of panic. "No! We've got to keep a lid on this!"

"Well, what are we going to do about her?" Vince stood from his chair pointed his thumb towards the front door. "The cat is out of the bag now. I've got to say something before we have press, cops, doctors, religious nuts… Oh, man."

"Oh, God in heaven. I've got to get out of here," Mr. Mercurio said quietly and rose from his chair. He spoke up as he headed up the stairs to his bedroom. "I'm packing a bag and going to Modesto! You call me at Uncle Rolf's after all this blows over!"

"What? Now?" Vince yelled back to him up the stairway. He shook his head in disbelief and turned back to Jerry. "Oh, well. At least I'll have the house to myself for the weekend. We should do this every Friday, huh?"

Jerry could only nod and laugh nervously. Vince bowed his head with his eyes closed for a moment and thought heavily. He looked up again, finished the coffee in the cup his father left on the table, and made his way for the front door. Jerry motioned feebly as if he wanted to stop him, but he backed down.

"Well, I've never been on TV before. That's a fine woman out there," he looked back at Jerry and grinned as he twisted the doorknob. "Maybe I can get her phone number."

Chapter Three

Jerry slipped back into the lab on Monday early to cover up his tracks. Methodically, he retraced his steps back to the point where he and Vince had stopped that Friday. First, he replaced the bottle of the V3 formula that he swiped and took home and then emptied the remaining bottles of V3 into an empty, one-gallon, plastic water jug and replaced each sample with leftover V2 formula. After the jug was stashed in the trunk of his car, he then threw out the regenerated samples in the bio-hazard disposal bins down the hall, marched back, and sat at one of the computer consoles. As he typed in the final bogus numbers from the night before into the lab records, Vince stepped in and smiled.

"Whoa," Vince laughed a bit and took off his sunglasses. "Mr. Spencer here beats me to the lab on a Monday for a change. Maybe I have died and gone to heaven after all."

Vince put his sunglasses into his inside coat pocket, put the coat on a nearby coat rack, and exchanged it for his usual white lab coat. He pinched himself on the back of his hand.

"I'm not dreaming either," he chuckled before finally noticed that Jerry was just about to close up the files on the lab computer. "What's all this then?"

"Oh, nothing...Nothing," Jerry muttered under his breath and pretended to remain nonchalant. He finished at the computer, stood up, and deliberately blocked the monitor from Vince's view, while he did his best to try to change the subject. "Umm... How'd the rest of the interviews go?"

"Fine, I guess," Vince said. "It was a nice follow up story to the shootout. I did a few more after Kate's aired, but I still think she and I had the best chemistry. Did you catch any of her stuff?"

"Umm…With Kate? I saw what little blurbs of it made it on the end of Sunday night's broadcast."

"Yeah, too bad about that tornado in Indiana," Vince sighed. "You can't blame them for knocking me out of the news cycle, but if I can milk this story, it might keep Dad out of the house a bit longer."

"So…" Jerry trailed off and began to feel more relieved. "Well, you might have had your moment in the spotlight come and go, but at least you got to meet Kate Lippold, eh? What's she really like?"

"Oooo. You might have to ask me about that one tomorrow morning," Vince smiled devilishly, lowered his head, looked up, and arched his eyebrows. "We're going to continue over dinner tonight. I'm thinking Guido's."

"Wha…What?" Jerry asked and left his mouth agape.

"Oh yes, you heard me," he continued. "God's re-gift to women actually has a date. I'm more surprised than you that I even had the courage to ask, much less that she said yes."

"A date?" Jerry asked.

"Well, I think she's really just interested in following up on the story," Vince said casually. "Maybe she's going to put a book together. Maybe she just needs a night out. Who cares? None of the other networks are following up on my story. Just another piece of local human interest time-filler."

"I guess in any other town, what happened to you might be considered weird." Jerry said.

"Still, a date's a date. Having been shot down by pretty women all my life, I usually have the intuition to know when they're out to get something. This time I'm not so sure. But what do I have to lose, right? It is Kate freaking Lippold were talking about here!" Vince laughed and started to work.

Jerry glanced at Vince sporadically out of the corner of his eye as they continued the lab's morning prep work, but he made sure that

Vince didn't notice him. Vince began whistling "Witchcraft" quietly but didn't notice as Jerry edged his way closer to him and tried to make out any other discernable changes.

"So," Jerry finally spoke again. "What did you do all day yesterday?"

"Ah, well. It was such a nice day, I went for a bike ride." Vince replied and took a new batch of samples out of one of the lab's refrigerators.

"A bike ride? Really?" Jerry asked.

"Yeah, I mean, look at this double chin!" Vince flexed his chin downward, which made his neck balloon a roll of fat out and forward. "I can't believe I'd let myself go like this for so long. I had to do something. So I went out and rode all day."

"How far did you get?" Jerry asked.

"Wow...Uhh...." Vince stopped what he was doing for a moment and recounted Sunday's ride. "Well, I checked out a lot of different places along the coast, but I think the farthest I got was the Palisades."

"Are you kidding me?" Jerry nearly coughed and his eyes bugged out in astonishment. "Aren't you even sore?"

"Nah, I'm OK. Even better. I didn't even need my inhaler. Maybe I'll be sore tomorrow," Vince continued and began to look at his first sample under a microscope. "I was on a roll. What can I say? Besides, what better time for yours truly to turn over a new leaf? If you can show up to work early on a Monday, then there's hope for us all."

The two of them grumbled and sunk their shoulders as they heard the tell tale clicking of Dr. Jacob's footsteps which echoed and grew louder as he approached from down the hall. Vince looked up from his microscope, narrowed his eyes a little, and turned around to face him just as he entered.

"Hey, it's Dr. J.!" Vince waved effeminately and gave him a coy smile. "And a very happy Monday to you."

The greeting stunned the otherwise unflappable Dr. Jacobs just enough for him to alter his constant stone faced expression and part his lips slightly as he contemplated a response. Just before he spoke, he tilted and rolled his balding head a little, as if half shrugging, this being what Vince and Jerry figured was a nervous muscle tick. Dr. Jacobs did this at least once or twice a day. But it was so obvious, that no one ever dared to mention it to him.

"Thank you, uhh…Mr. Mercurio," Dr. Jacobs replied in his usual cold, calculating tone. "I heard about your little, uhh… Mishap over the weekend and I hope this will not further erode your typical job performance here."

"What, that?" Vince smirked and leaned against his workstation. "Happens to me all the time, really. I feel great. Plus, I can see dead people now. Can't wait to start the W series, boss."

"Huh," Dr. Jacobs muttered to himself. He paused, remained still, but his eyes leered between Vince and Jerry for a while. Jerry finally looked up from his microscope, took a couple quick glances at Vince, and smiled nervously while he tried to remain casual. He focused on Jerry, took off his thick-framed glasses, and asked, "Did you finish filing the results of the V-series?"

"Oh, yes!" Jerry responded with enthusiasm at first, and then lowered his voice, "Umm… I mean, yes, Dr. Jacobs. Everything is logged in and… Uhh… As it should be. Yes."

"Huh," Dr. Jacobs muttered once more. He detected that Jerry's breath grew deeper and measured and his eyes avoided contact with his. Looking back at Vince, he saw him continue to lean on his workstation, calm and cheerful. Dr. Jacobs backed away towards the door as if he was about to leave which made Jerry relax a little, but Jerry stiffened up again when he turned back to them and spoke. "Look, not that your work is interesting to me in the slightest, but Harlan Mansell is here today. Michael has a deep personal interest in the project and this kid asked to shadow here in our labs for a while. For some reason, and against my recommendation I might add, he asked that his only child be shacked up with you two."

"Well, at least our work is interesting to somebody." Vince said with arms folded and a satisfied grin. Dr. Jacobs had almost lost his patience with Vince entirely when the three of them heard footsteps approaching from outside the lab. Dr. Jacobs peered outside the door and waved down the hall. While his back was turned, Jerry looked accusingly at Vince.

"Dr. J.?" Jerry whispered under his breath, just before Dr. Jacobs turned back to face them again.

"Alright, Harlan's here," Dr. Jacobs tightened his jaw and spoke softly, but menacingly through his teeth. "Just answer questions and be polite. Now, do you think you two can handle that?"

Jerry nodded nervously while Vince just gave him a playful salute and continued to grin. Just before Dr. Jacobs could react, Harlan Mansell entered the lab. At first they looked up almost a foot too high, before Jerry and Vince looked down to see that Harlan was not only just under five feet tall, but also a pretty, young woman with long blond hair in a ponytail. She approached them first, took off her thick glasses, and gave them a wide smile.

"Oh-h-h, hi-i-i!" her mousy, breathy voice stretched out each word as she extended her hand to Jerry first. Jerry's eyes lit up as she drew closer, but he extended his hand to hers almost reluctantly. His eyes locked into hers as she took his limp hand and shook it warmly.

"I thought you were a man." Her hand still in his, Jerry's words passed unconsciously at first. Two seconds later, his face cringed as he realized what he had said. Behind her, Jerry could see Dr. Jacobs was glaring at him. Vince simply chuckled quietly to himself and slightly shook his head.

"Oh, that's fine," she giggled and let his hand go. "I get that a lot. Please, call me Lonnie!"

"I will!" Jerry blurted a little too loudly, and then piped down and cleared his throat. She turned to Vince who was already stepping forward.

"Lonnie Mansell."

"Vince, how you doing?" he asked jovially and shook her hand.

"Great. So this is the place. Nice. I look forward to working with you two," she giggled a little again, and then faced Dr. Jacobs and whispered quietly. "I've… Uhh… Just got to freshen up a bit. Where's?"

Dr. Jacobs simply nodded and whispered back, "Follow me."

"Umm, I'll be right back," she said to Vince and Jerry. "Stay put."

Vince and Jerry waited till he could hear both Lonnie and Dr. Jacobs march far enough away. Vince could see Jerry's accusing eyes as they leveled into his.

"What?" Vince said and turned his hands up.

"What the hell is she doing?" Jerry whispered loudly.

"Look, Jerry. All girls go to the bathroom, right? I thought you knew this."

Too anxious to recognize his sarcasm, Jerry just stared at him. Vince rubbed one of his temples and took a deep breath.

"Come on, man. Lighten up. This is great!" he laughed and gave Jerry a pat on the shoulder. "It's Mansell's daughter! You know I'm totally jealous now. You know it! But I'm a man of honor, and I've already got dibs on Kate, so don't mess this up."

"Up? Uh, what?" Jerry stammered but couldn't follow him.

"This is it, man!" Vince congratulated him. "She's rich. She's new in town. She's totally into you!"

"Me? What? You're crazy!" Jerry struggled to answer. "She sounds like she's been taking bong hits! Nobody that rich is ever that nice to guys like us."

"Like us? What are you talking about? You've just hit the jack-pot!" Vince insisted.

"Why is she here? Who would give a rat's ass about anything we do here? Of all the labs in the company, why us?" Jerry's face stiffened as Vince's grew relaxed.

"Well, you'll just have to ask her when she comes back, now won't you?" Vince grinned, folded his arms again, and leaned back on one of the counters. "Relax, man. You've been acting all weird since Friday. Are you sure you weren't the one who was struck by lightning?"

"Well, I! I mean, she! God! I watched you die that night!" Jerry started to pace around nervously. With his back turned to Vince, he did his best to control his panic. "Sorry. It's just; I'm still a little shook. I did every thing I could to save you, but I..." There was a long pause, but Vince eventually broke the silence.

"You, uh...." Vince hesitated as he spoke. "Tried mouth-to-mouth, right?"

"Yeah." Jerry turned back to him.

"Eww. Nasty," Vince said through his teeth and wriggled a little. "I hope you brushed your teeth first."

"That's not funny!" he shot back. "You would have done it for me!"

"The hell I would have." Vince chuckled.

"I! Wait!" Jerry stopped and heard the sound of Lonnie's footsteps, as they grew louder from down the hall. He did his best to regain what little composure he still had and whispered to Jerry just before Lonnie came in. "Just...Just...Don't say anything stupid."

Lonnie looked up as she stepped through the door, closed her handbag, and smiled dreamily. "Oh, hi. Me again. Thanks for waiting."

Without missing a beat, Vince pointed his finger at Jerry and announced, "Jerry here was just asking what a classy young lady like you is doing in a lab like this."

"Oh, you did?" she responded and blushed from the flattery.

Jerry's eye's widened and he smiled through his clenched jaw while he feigned laughter, "Ha. Uhh... Well maybe in not... Uhh... So many words, but I... It's just with the diversity of your fath-... Umm... I mean, the company. I just wondered what in particular attracted you to... Uhh... This... Place."

"Well, I thought working in R & D would be a nice change of pace," Lonnie said, put her handbag down, and straightened her glasses. Her casual reaction to Jerry eased his anxiety slightly. "I was just getting so bored with the company business and the east coast society scene. I'd never been to California and I thought the work here would be a nice way to get my hands dirty."

"First time, huh? Really?" Vince asked.

"Um-hmm," she smiled and nodded.

"Well, that's great! Jerry here is a native Angelino, born and raised, he is," Vince put his arm around his shoulder, but Jerry remained stiff as a board. "I'm sure he'd be more than happy to give you a grand tour."

"Uhh... What?" Jerry was still too stiff to pay his full attention.

"Yeah, just show her all the big ones. Take her to the beach," Vince stepped away and inhaled deeply, while he looked out the lab's window. "It's a beautiful day out there. Hit Hollywood Boulevard, the Tar Pits, the Getty, Griffith. You know where to go."

Jerry didn't know how to answer, so he simply smiled and waited nervously for Lonnie to say something. She paused for a couple seconds with her hands at her sides, then smiled again and nodded.

"Yeah, that actually sounds nice."

"No!" Jerry blurted out and then quickly lowered his voice, "Sorry... Uhh... I mean, we've got work to finish today and I wouldn't want you to get in trouble on your first day, and-"

"What? Give me a break," Vince cut in and laughed. "It's the daughter of the boss! What is Jacobs going to do? Fire you?"

"Really, I'd appreciate it. My treat!" Lonnie said sweetly.

"Come on, Jer'," Vince walked between Lonnie and Jerry, put an arm around each of their shoulders, and led them to the door. Lonnie picked up her coat and handbag again. "I'll get started on this batch and we'll cram tomorrow, OK?"

"Yeah, but…" Jerry weakly tried to speak.

"Sounds great!" Lonnie spoke up just before Jerry could utter another syllable. "Thanks, Vince."

"No problem. Have fun, kids." Vince winked at Jerry, who tried to say something again, but Vince gently pushed them out and shut the door. The sound of the door shutting echoed down the hallway. Jerry barely had a moment to think about going for the doorknob again, when he heard the sound of Vince locking it before he could touch it. He could see the silhouette of Vince behind the frosted glass windowpane on the door and Jerry motioned to speak, but stopped as the silhouette slipped away. He spun around and faced Lonnie, but was at a loss for words.

"OK," she said after a long pause. "Where'd you park?"

Chapter Four

A wave swept in and enveloped Lonnie's bare feet. She let out a high-pitched shriek and giggled as she ran back towards Jerry onto the dry sand. She held her shoes and socks in one hand, and beckoned him towards her with the other.

"Come on!" she yelled over the roaring surf of Venice Beach. "It's colder than I thought it would be, but it feels great! Take your shoes off!"

"Umm… OK," Jerry relented and started to take off his shoes and socks. He pointed towards the boardwalk and shouted back to her as another wave rolled in. "But we really should wash our feet off at one of showers when we're done! That water's totally filled with mercury and God knows what!"

"Yeah, yeah, yeah. Get over here!"

He took his shoes and socks in one hand and rolled up his pant legs, clenched his jaw, and started to move towards her.

"Here goes," he muttered to himself. Another wave rolled in and his eyes bugged out as it came up to his ankles. He pounced out of the cool water like a cat and ran back to the dry sand. "Wow! You weren't kidding!"

"Come on! It's not that bad after you've been in for a few seconds!" she shouted and playfully kicked up some water at him.

Jerry flinched, but the splash missed, and he pretended to laugh. He nodded nervously, took a deep breath, and took cautious steps toward the water again. Another wave came in and he braced himself and took intense, shallow breaths through his nostrils as the cool water caressed his skin once more.

"Whoa! Ahhh. Yeah, that is nice," Jerry squinted from the bright glare that reflected off the water. He scanned along the shore ahead of them. "Keep an eye out for hypodermic needles too. We are barefoot."

"Okie-dokie," She replied and they started walking down the beach parallel to the water. "Now I've officially put my feet in the water at Venice, Italy, Florida, and California."

"There are better beaches I could take you to," he said. "Though I admit it looks nicer than I remember."

"When was the last time you were out here?" she asked.

"Oooo." he scratched his head, paused, and then started to walk again. "Since, err... Vince and I were roommates at UCLA, I think. Going on five years now, dang."

"You've been friends that long?"

"Oh, yeah," He nodded and checked out the scenery. "He got me into science. Uhh, there's a lot of ground we need to cover if you want to see all the things you wanted to today. How much longer do you want to stay here?"

Lonnie shielded her eyes with her hand, peered down the shore, and pointed.

"Umm. We'll walk to the guy with the stunt kite. Then we'll head back. OK?" she replied and he nodded. "Vince is a funny guy. You two must have had some wild times down here back in the day, huh?"

"I like to think that I was the wilder one then. I got Vince outdoors and introduced him to people and he paid me back, getting me through college." Jerry said.

"Bad grades?"

"Nah. Well, yes at first," he admitted. "I was undeclared and unmotivated. I thought business in the beginning, get rich quick and all, but I hated it. I've always had an aptitude for science, just never really pursued it. Vince was already in to neuroscience, so he talked me through it, and the rest is history. I'd still like to be rich someday. What's it like?"

"Oh, probably more boring than you think," she said. "Talk about being unmotivated. That and having to grow up under dad's shadow. I wanted to start at the bottom. I want to feel like I can accomplish something on my own, really earn something for once."

"Well, the bottom's where I'm at." he laughed slightly. Another wave rolled in, farther than before, which caught them both by surprise, and soaked them up to the thighs.

"*AH!*" Lonnie shrieked and they ran back onto the beach as the wave receded. Lonnie gasped, hugged Jerry, jumped up and down, and giggled hysterically. Jerry caught his breath, but was taken aback by Lonnie's hyperactive behavior. "Oh, Jerry! I can't tell you the last time I have had this much fun! Come on! I'll race you to the kite guy!"

"Uhh." he cocked his head a little and put his hands on his hips.

"In 3, 2, 1." she said, and then took off running.

"Oh, boy." Jerry muttered to himself and chased after her. She was already way in front by the time he took off, but he did his best to catch up. Feeling his old competitive streak kick in once again, he charged through another wave as it rolled in and made his thighs even wetter. He almost caught up to her, but she beat him to the man with the kite.

"Ha! I won! I get to decide where ne-e-ext!" she playfully sang her words and skipped around, which startled the kite guy. After he caught up, Jerry struggled to catch his breath and rested his hands on his knees.

"OK.... OK..." he panted and then gulped. "Where to now?"

"How about..." she scratched her head and paused, "Let's hit Hollywood and that Chinese Theater."

"Alright, but uhh..." he inhaled deeply through his nose. "If we run into the guy in the Barney suit at the Theater, I've got to lay low. We had a little scuffle last time I was there."

Across town, Vince and Kate had just finished their generous plates of pasta at Guido's. A couple bites short, Kate leaned back, slumped into her chair, and put her silverware down on her plate. She smiled despite how stuffed she was.

"Oh my God," she exhaled through her plump, puckered lips. "That was **GOOD**. But I'm afraid I'm down for the count."

Vince nodded in agreement and grunted hungrily as he polished off the last bite on his plate. He took a deep breath and calmly placed his silverware on his plate as well. As he leaned forward, Vince placed his elbows on the table and smiled knowingly.

"What?" she asked.

"Oh, I saved the best for last," he replied and flagged down the waiter. As the waiter cleared their dinner plates, Vince leaned back in his chair, tented his fingers, and very politely asked, "Sir, will you please bring us each an order of your tiramisu?"

"What? Oh no! I can't," she insisted. The waiter looked to Vince for approval. He nodded, gave him a thumbs up, and a wink. The waiter smiled, nodded, and returned to the kitchen with their empty plates. "Are you nuts?", she asked as she embraced her full belly.

"Mmm. Probably. You know, I've been getting asked that a lot lately," he said casually and leaned forward in his chair. "I'll make you a deal. You take one bite. One. And if you can't go on, I promise you, I will not only finish mine, but I'll be more than happy to finish yours."

"It's that good, huh?" she asked.

"Oh yeah." Vince replied and his voice went an octave deeper.

"You are going to wreck my career, you know," she joked. "My guess is that you are secretly working for another network. Seriously, I will suffer for this. Do you know what I have to go through to stay in this shape?"

"My dear, this city adores you. Take it from me," he reassured her. "If anything, a couple extra pounds will only gain you more fans."

"Oh yeah, like who?"

"The one's too jealous of your figure to like you, for starters." he added.

"Oh, yeah right," she chuckled. "Let me make anchor first. Then at least my audience won't be able to see me below the waist. Ugh, this business. That's all I've been talking about all night. Me. You've been so patient, listening to all my stupid complaints. I still know hardly anything about you."

"Well, before I met you, my life really wasn't that interesting." he smiled.

"Aw, come on."

"Really," Vince rested his chin in his hand, and looked up, and reflected. "My life before I got zapped. I remember everything so clearly, yet it feels as if... Oh, I don't know. It's like it happened to somebody else, somebody different."

"How so?"

"I see this young man," he continued. "Carrying on so single mindedly, so driven to excel in his work. By the way, he was **VERY** good at it too. But he had nothing else. He denied himself so much of life's pleasures, that at some point, he could only find pleasure in denying himself pleasure."

"Huh," Kate's eyes locked into his. "So what does this new young man want now?"

"Nothing but good times."

They shared a few seconds of silence, and stared at each other with satisfied grins, when they were both startled by the ringing of Vince's cell phone. Vince chuckled and rose from his chair.

"Oh Jerry, Jerry, Jerry," he sighed. "Sorry, honey. He's panicking about something. I'll be right back. This shouldn't take a second."

Kate nodded and gave him an OK sign with her hand. Vince answered his cell phone as he stepped out to the front, but kept sight of Kate through the restaurant's window.

"Oh boy. This better be good," Vince said and listened calmly to

Jerry as he ranted on the other end. "Alright, alright, alright. Chill out now, tiger. What is it? Uh huh... Uh huh... She wants to try karaoke? Well take her there then...What do you mean, you can't go there alone?... I got news for you, bubba, you are on a **DATE**... OK, OK, OK, fine. We're just finishing here anyway. We'll come join you."

Vince saw the waiter bring the two plates of tiramisu to their table, and smiled widely at Kate as she took her first bite. Her eyes bugged out in amazement as she swallowed it and went to take another bite.

"See? Told ya'," he mumbled to himself, and then focused again on Jerry. "What? No, not you. Look, where are you guys now? Uh huh... OK. I think I know a place nearby."

"The Brass Monkey?" Dave Liebowitz said through his Bluetooth phone as he raced down the street in his vintage, silver Porsche convertible. "Where the hell is that? On Wilshire? Next to what? OK, OK, OK, fine."

He pumped his brakes as a white SUV abruptly cut in front of him and he leaned heavily on his horn.

"Awful jackass!" he grinded his teeth and lowered his voice. "Can't you just call a cab?... Why do I have to be there now? Never mind. I'll be there in five. I've gotta go. Rick's on the other line." Dave clicked a button on his dashboard and he continued, "Rick! What is it? ... Uh huh... Uh huh... What? ... No, not again! ... I thought you finalized that tour rider agreement with them! What happened? ... They want what? ... Where the hell are you going to find Tahitian Treat in freakin' Poland? ... Look, I... I don't care! ... Tell them to stop acting like children and be professionals, for God's sake! ... I could care less what they like to mix with it! Just deal with it, OK!?! I've gotta go... Yeah, bye!"

Dave hit his fist briskly once on the dashboard and shook his head to himself in disbelief. The tires of his car squeaked short, but loudly as he shoved his brake pedal, and halted behind a couple cars at a stoplight. He grumbled, opened his glove compartment, took out a small prescription medicine bottle, and furiously tried to pry open the child protected lid. It finally popped off, but his shaking, nerve wracked hands flung the tablets all over the interior of his car.

"God damn it!" he shouted which caught the attention of the commuters surrounding him. While he attempted to regain his cool, Dave clenched his jaws, and searched around for a couple of the tablets. Finding two resting on his shirt, he picked them off, unclenched his jaw, and swallowed them immediately. His throat struggled a moment to pass the tablets through without anything to wash them down. Dave was too stressed out to care about the discomfort. The light turned green again and he muttered to himself as he hit the gas, "What a bunch of schmuck amateurs."

He weaved through the traffic until he made it to the Brass Monkey. His wife Jodi was waiting and eagerly waved him into a parking space in front.

"Come on! Come on! Get inside!" she shouted at him.

Dave turned off the ignition, put on the parking brake, got out, and started to put up the Porsche's convertible cloth roof.

"Don't worry about the roof! Just follow me!" she took his hand and yanked him inside.

"I swear, Jodi, this is the last time I let you go on a bachlorette's party," he said as they went inside and the door shut behind them.

Dave became spellbound the microsecond he heard Vince's voice. Vince had just wrapped up the last verse of his second song, "I Got You Under My Skin". Despite his long career in the music business, the sheer beauty of Vince's smooth delivery instantly melted away decades of his icy cynicism. All the eyes of Jodi's bachlorette party, Jerry, Lonnie, Kate, and the staff of the Brass Monkey were firmly fixed on stage and they were all speechless as well until he finished the song with a meteoric crescendo.

The entire place erupted in applause as Vince punctuated the last note with a "Yeah!" Dave's ecstasy turned to panic the moment he noticed that several of Jodi's friends had recorded the performance on their camera phones.

"No, no, no, no, no", he jabbered anxiously and he turned to his wife. "Oh, God! They haven't posted any of this stuff yet, have they?"

"Sure. We're telling everybody we know," she replied cheerfully, and then her expression turned to puzzlement as Dave began to search through her purse. "What's wrong? What do you think are you doing?"

"How much money do you have?" he whispered desperately.

"What?" she asked.

"How much!" he demanded and then piped down. "Give me everything you have. Now. Don't ask. Just do it."

Jodi wrestled her purse back from him and calmly found the pocket that had her cash and gave him a handful of bills.

"Here. There's a little over a hundred dollars there. Happy?"

On stage, Vince thumbed through the karaoke songbook and smiled as the rest of the place pleaded for another song. The crowd begged for more until his eyes finally lit up and Vince pointed to a line in the book as he handed it to the karaoke operator. "OK, one more and I'm done tonight," he said to the audience through the microphone. A chorus of boos and pleads for him to continue followed. "I know, I know, but I'm being rude to my date. I'll do one more and that's only because I like you."

Vince waited until the notes of "Black Magic" started coming through the speakers. Dave tried desperately to stay focused, not to be mesmerized by Vince's voice, as he rifled through his pockets, digging up whatever money he had. He counted the money with trembling fingers, furrowed his brow a little, and glanced around the room. His eyes spotted an ATM machine in the corner, so he power walked over to it and took three hundred dollars out of it as fast as he could. After he marched back to his wife, he slowly steadied himself to really listen and become entranced by Vince once again.

Vince made his way into the crowd as far as the microphone cord would allow him as he playfully sang to each of Jodi's friends. One by one, as he sang to them, the women would begin to swoon and fan themselves with their hands or whatever they could find. Vince saved the final verse for Kate as he sashayed close to her. Their eyes sparkled from the clubs lights while he took her hand and sat at their table. Lonnie and Jerry sat across the table. Lonnie swooned like the other women, but Jerry was completely frozen and speechless. Vince gave Kate a quick, soft peck on her hand as he rose from his chair and stepped back on stage and gave the audience one last big finish.

Everybody leapt to their feet and applauded. Vince took a bow, smiled, waved his hands for a couple seconds, and walked back to his table. Jodi and her friends burst into a cacophony of laugher and praise, while they edged their way forward. Vince had almost sat down when Dave slipped in next to him and beckoned them to get back.

"Now, now, ladies," he said loudly, but cheerfully. "There's no need to crowd the man. Just a moment." He turned again to Vince and put out his hand to shake. "Well done there, sir. That was amazing. My name is Dave Liebowitz."

"Why thank you. Vince Mercurio." Vince replied, shook his hand, and sat down.

"I don't want to keep you from your evening. I just wanted to give you this," Dave said and reached into his coat pocket, giving him his business card, along with almost five hundred dollars in a wad of folded bills. "That's just a little retainer for your time right now. But if you come by my office and listen to what I have to say tomorrow, I'll give you five thousand dollars. And you can keep that money whether you like what I propose or not."

"Five G? On the level, just for showing up?" Vince's expression lit up as he took the card and money.

"On the level."

"I've got to work tomorrow, but I can be there by six. Is that OK?"

Vince put the money into his coat pocket, but held onto the business card and examined it.

"Six is fine," Dave replied instantly. "I'll see you then. Good night everybody. Enjoy the rest of your evening."

He politely smiled and waved, turned around, found his wife, and gently took her by the arm. She resisted at first. "Trust me, Jodi. Let's roll now. If everything works out like I want, you'll be seeing a lot more of this kid."

Jodi nodded reluctantly. She said goodbye to her friends and walked out with Dave. Back at Vince's table, they passed around the business card.

"None of you guys follow music, do you?" Kate asked.

"Not really", Lonnie said. "I'm more into classical."

"Not anything really new in a while", Jerry said.

"Just the oldies, baby." Vince said.

"Well, I know that this guy is one of the biggest music producers in the world, not just this town," Kate said. "There are people in this town who would kill you for that card there."

"Well, I won't go without my personal manager." Vince laughed and patted Jerry on the shoulder.

"What?" Jerry said in disbelief.

"Our ships come in, my friend." Vince said and beamed.

"I don't know anything about the music industry."

"But I can trust you. And I know enough about the industry to know that you're worth your weight in gold," Vince said. The words stunned Jerry and Vince went on. "Just come with me tomorrow. You'll get fifteen percent."

"Ten percent." Jerry said instinctually. "I'm just your manager."

"Agent's get ten. Managers get fifteen," Vince shot back and patted him on the shoulder again. "See. I can trust you *AND* your not greedy. Now you're worth twenty times your weight in gold. You're exactly what I need."

Chapter Five

The light was on in the living room as Vince pulled up to his house. He half grinned, turned off the ignition, and got out of the car.

"Oh, good. Papa's home. Surprise, surprise," he said quietly to himself. "Knew my luck couldn't go on forever."

He locked up the car and walked up to the front door to find it unlocked. Vince hadn't even shut the door behind him when his father sprung up from an easy chair in the living room and confronted him.

"Where the hell have you been?" Mr. Mercurio demanded. "Do you know what time it is? Is that *MY* suit you're wearing?"

"Whoa! Whoa. Whoa. Slow down. One at a time," Vince put his hands up and made an effort to calm his father down. He counted to three on one hand as he answered. "I was on a date with Kate," He looked at his wristwatch. "It's exactly 1:04 in the morning and yes, it is your suit, though these are my shoes, socks, and underwear."

"You…" Vince's cool response only bewildered him further. Mr. Mercurio clenched his fists and took a step closer. "You went on a *DATE* with her? Why?!"

"What do mean 'Why'? She was hot!" Vince laughed, took off his coat, and draped it over one of the living room chairs. He loosened his tie, walked into the kitchen, and poured himself a tall glass of water. He took a long drink, and nearly finished the glass, and then continued. "Hey, I didn't grill you about what you did with Uncle Rolf this weekend."

"This is *MY* house!" he pointed accusingly. "And while you live under this roof you'll-"

"OK, OK, OK!" Vince interrupted. "I get it! I won't raid your wardrobe again. Look, here." He put down the glass, kicked off his shoes, and took his pants off.

"Wha-...What are you doing?" Mr. Mercurio asked.

"I'll even pay for the dry cleaning," Vince folded the pants neatly and placed them on top of the coat on the chair. He whipped the tie off his collar and started unbuttoning his shirt. "Now will you lay off?"

"I don't care about the suit!" Mr. Mercurio said. "I don't want you seeing that damn reporter!"

"Are you kidding?" Vince scoffed dismissively, shook his head, and unbuttoned his cuffs. After he finally got his shirt off, he placed it on the chair, and faced his father in his underwear and socks. "Are you totally blind now? Do I have to spell it out for you? Kate is hot! *H-O-T*! She's totally crazy about me! I had her eating out of my hand tonight!"

"Oh my God," Mr. Mercurio went pale, paced a little, and had to sit down. "This can't be happening."

"What?" Vince asked. "That I'm actually doing something with my life? That I'm running the risk of enjoying sex with a beautiful woman?"

"I just... It's just..." Mr. Mercurio stammered. "I just want you to be safe, that's all."

"Safe? Safe is boring, Dad. Look what safe had gotten me before this," Vince started to walk up the stairs. "Now I've got to be up for work in a few hours and I've got a big day tomorrow." Mr. Mercurio turned in his chair and almost spoke, but was stunned upon what his son said just before he closed the door to his bedroom upstairs. "I'll tell you about my new music career later."

Ayman Mohammed paced around his apartment clearly agitated while he talked to his girlfriend on the phone. He even contemplated smoking a cigarette for the first time in a month out of an emergency pack he had stashed in his nightstand.

"Baby, baby, baby. Why are you doing this?" he pleaded and shook his head. "What?… Why now?… Look, I know it's been slow for a while, but that's just the business, honey. It'll turn around any day now. It always has. It always does."

Ayman tried in vain to get a word in for almost a minute. Every time he tried to speak, he was stopped before he could get out a single syllable. He finally gave in and took a smoke from his emergency pack, lit it, took a long drag, and continued to pace. Suddenly his pacing stopped.

"What?!" he blurted out loudly. He heard a thumping on his floor from the downstairs neighbor. "OK, OK, OK!" he shouted and stomped his foot once to acknowledge his neighbor's displeasure. He lowered his voice, but began to seethe with resentment, "You went **BACK** to him? After the way he treated you? What the hell for? … What? … You can depend on him? Depend on him? You can depend on him for treating you like a god damn slave! You… You… What? … Who cares if he's managing the Best Buy now? The guy's a total creep! How do you think this makes me feel? … Your feelings? … Oh now it's about your feelings? Didn't I treat you like a lady? … No, no, no! How can you do this to me now, baby? Is money really that important to- Hello? Hello?"

He looked at the display on his phone and threw it down on his bed.

"She hung up," he said to himself and started to pace around the room again. He puffed furiously on his cigarette. "Damn. No way. No way. This can't be for real. Stupid girl…. She'll be back. Oh yeah, a week or two of that dork and she'll come crawling back. I know her."

A few seconds later, his phone rang again. He was so startled that he nearly knocked over a tall African wood figure sculpture on his nightstand when he swung around. He dropped the cigarette out of his hand and fumbled around with the teetering sculpture until he grasped it firmly and set it upright again. Ayman picked up the cigarette again and took one last long drag before he picked up the phone. He walked to his kitchen sink, put out the cigarette under the faucet, and let the phone ring one last time before answering.

"Damn, that was faster than I thought," he said to himself. Smugly, he put the phone to his ear and spoke into it again. "What? You got something else to say to me now?... What? Dave? ... Dave is that you? ... Do you know what time it- ... Never mind... Tomorrow? We haven't spoken in five years and you want me to-... Uhh, I'm at the studio tomorrow with Kevin... Yeah, my studio. I'm still in the same one. Yeah sure. We still play with Troy sometimes... The hell if I know what he's doing tomorrow."

He walked back into the kitchen, opened the sliding glass door, and stepped out to the balcony overlooking downtown LA. His expression changed to amazement.

"*10 G*??! Each?! Just for one day? Are you screwing with me?" he blurted loudly, but then piped down, worried that he would upset his neighbor again. "Man, Dave. You haven't relapsed, have you? ... You don't sound drunk. More like you're tweekin'... OK, OK. I believe you... Swing stuff? Yeah, sure. How can we forget? All those corporate gigs in the 90's got us all paid when it was in, but why now? ... Uh huh... So he's that good, huh? God almighty singing couldn't impress you and this guy did?"

Ayman walked back inside and found his address book, flipped through a few pages, and found the number for Troy Nixon. He still couldn't believe what he was hearing.

"OK. That's 10 G each, right?" he said as he double-checked with Dave. "Yeah, I'll call him next. You've already booked time with Pete? Damn, you are serious. Alright, we'll be in around four and you say this guy... Uhh, Vince will be in around six? ... Yeah, that should give us enough time to warm up about eight or nine songs. You're buying dinner though, got it?... Whatever we want? Dave, you weren't visited by three ghosts last night by chance, were you? ... OK, whatever, man. You better be there... Uh huh. Yeah. See ya'."

He hung up and walked back out to his balcony. His eyes squinted in the dim light as he pressed the digits of Troy Dixon's phone number and waited for him to answer. He fidgeted and paced back and forth till Troy picked up after the fifth ring.

"Troy?" he asked. "Yeah, it's me. Sorry I'm calling you so late, but man, you are *NOT* going to believe this. What are you doing tomorrow?"

Chapter Six

Vince spotted Jerry just about to enter the front door of Mansell Labs and he blew him a sharp whistle. Jerry's head whipped around, which brought back the slight kink in his neck he received the previous Saturday. Jerry rubbed it after finally seeing Vince in the distance. They waved to each other from across the parking lot and Jerry waited until he caught up with him.

"Hey, what's up, man?" Vince shook his hand and patted him on the back as they went inside and strolled towards their lab. "Last night had to be the best night of my life, next to losing my virginity. Hell, and that was so long ago, I barely remember that one. So did you score?"

"Vince! I just met her." Jerry responded sourly.

"So what? She was all over you. Ah, you're probably right," he said as they turned a corner. "Gotta be a gent, right? I just got a smooch from Kate myself, but boy howdy! That one hit me harder than the lightning."

Having walked in the building, they made it to their lab, and swung open the door, and saw that Dr. Jacobs was looking over their files at their workstation. They gave each other a quick, puzzled glance, and then looked back as Dr. Jacobs rose from his chair and cleared his throat.

"Finally, you're here," he said and looked sternly at a clock on the wall. "I've been going over your findings from the SW formula and I think it looks promising. I need you two to go over the series again."

"Again?! Oh man." Vince muttered quietly, shook his head, and exchanged his coat for his lab coat off the coat rack.

"We…Uhh…We already went over that data, sir," Jerry went

pale with terror, but held it together. "I mean, really, the V-series yielded no significant changes than the T or the U series for that matter."

"I don't care," Dr. Jacobs said bluntly. "You two must start every series again and under my personal supervision this time."

"Aw, great," Vince folded his arms and sneered. "A whole month with Dr. J. breathing down our necks."

"Don't ever call me Dr. J. again," he growled back. "And we don't have a month. This has to be done by the end of the week."

"A week?!", Jerry and Vince said simultaneously.

"So I guess you'll be putting in some overtime. Lucky you." Dr. Jacobs said.

"Nah-nah-nah-nah," Vince said rapidly. "I'm outta here at five. I already got plans."

"Well, you're going to cancel them, aren't you?" Dr. Jacobs demanded. They stared each other down for a few seconds as Jerry glanced nervously at the both of them. Vince let out a long sigh, closed his eyes for a moment, and then slowly took off his lab coat.

"What do you think you're doing?" Dr. Jacobs asked.

"Two weeks notice, Dr. J.," Vince replied, cool as a cucumber, and he put his lab coat back on the coat rack. "Oh, and I'm feeling kind of woozy, so I think I'm going to use up my sick days for the next two weeks as well. I think it must be from the lightning, or maybe it's that lousy coffee from the cafeteria."

Jerry and Dr. Jacobs were too stunned to speak as Vince put on his regular coat and headed for the door, but it opened just before he could reach the handle. Lonnie was on the other side and she let out a sudden, high-pitched eek noise and then giggled.

"Oh, hi Vince!" she said and walked in. Her eyeglasses had slid down her nose a bit from the startle and she pushed them back up with her index finger. "What's going on?"

"Not much. I just quit," Vince said casually. Lonnie gasped as

Vince turned to Jerry. "So, you coming or not? You're still my manager, remember?"

"Uhh…Uhh…" Jerry stammered.

"It's cool. You don't have to decide right away," Vince said as he walked out. They could hear him still talking as he walked out of sight the way he came. "Just pop by that studio at six if you're still interested!"

There was an uncomfortable silence for a few seconds until Jerry finally broke it.

"Look, umm. I'm sorry Dr. J., I mean, Dr. Jacobs," Jerry said nervously. "I think I'm feeling kind of woozy too. Better turn in my notice. It looks like this might be contagious."

"Jerry!" Lonnie whined.

"I'm so sorry, hon'. I've got to do this," he said as he put his hands on her shoulders. They hugged and then he turned away. As Jerry walked out the door, he stopped and faced her again. "Uhh… You still have my number, right?"

"Uh-huh", she responded and grew sad.

"Great. Well, I'd like to see you again. I mean, I…" he glanced over to Dr. Jacobs, whose face grew red while he barely contained his fury. "Uhh, yeah. I better go."

Lonnie pouted and motioned to speak as Jerry made a quick exit. Dr. Jacobs did one of his nervous neck ticks as Lonnie folded her arms and her mood turned bitter. She gave him a threatening look.

"What?" Dr. Jacobs responded in bemusement unable to completely control his rage.

"No way, Kate." Jack Fulmer answered bluntly in his low, gravelly voice. Another reporter walked in from the bustling newsroom, dropped some papers on his desk, and left again.

"Come on, Jack." Kate pleaded.

"No," he said flatly and continued to scan over the papers on his desk. "This kind of story is beneath you. I mean, who cares? The mayors screwing around again and I want you and that goldbricker Jim down at City Hall in a half an hour."

"But you should have heard him," she said as her hopes sank. "It was like nothing I've ever heard. This is weird, even for LA."

"I don't care," he insisted, but still didn't look at her. "Leave this kind of fluff for Entertainment Tonight or Fox News. Look, I admire your dedication here. I do. But you know better than to get this emotionally involved. It's unprofessional."

"What?!" she demanded.

"Besides, if I gave every reporter at this station free reign to put their boyfriend's on the air-", he chuckled before being interrupted.

"-He's **NOT**..." she spoke up and then lowered her voice so the others in the studio couldn't hear. "He's not my boyfriend, Jack. He... Umm... He..."

Jack finally slouched his shoulders and looked up at her with his large puppy dog eyes. Kate folded her arms in frustration.

"OK, he isn't ... yet." she admitted.

"Uh-huh," He looked back down at his papers. "Kate, you're a human when you're off the clock, but here you're a journalist and I'm in charge. Do you get me?"

"City Hall?" she asked and nodded reluctantly.

"Mmm-hmm," he replied. "Get going. Take Van 2."

Pete Sanders sat motionless, except for the miniscule adjustments he made to the faders on his enormous mixing board with his fingertips, as Vince and the band finished the last couple bars of "Stepping Out" in the studio. Dave and Jerry stood right behind Pete in the control room, all three gazing at Vince through the thick plexiglass until a few seconds of silence passed.

"Tell me you got that." Dave said finally snapped out of his gaze.

Pete gently pressed a button on the keyboard that controlled his hard drive.

"Oh yeah." Pete grinned as he took off the band holding his long grey ponytail. He let his hair fall over his shoulders and he quickly took a joint out of a metal mint case on the console and lit it.

"In all your years in this lousy business have you ever-..." Dave found himself at a loss of words.

"Never." Pete inhaled deeply and continued to gaze at Vince, who laughed and shook hands with the band, though their voices were muffled on the other side of the glass. Dave leaned over Pete and pressed a buttoned labeled 'God Mic' on the console.

"Excellent work, boys!" he smiled and waved to them. "I think we've got everything we need tonight. Why don't we leave the gear for now and we'll celebrate over some dinner and drinks? OK?"

Vince and the band all smiled, nodded, and gave various hand signs in approval.

"Every take, Dave. Every single damn one," Pete said and offered his joint to Jerry, who politely declined. Pete took another drag and spoke as he held it in. "Perfect. I mean, the mix down will hardly be necessary. We might as well go ahead and master this baby now."

"Well, definitely burn some copies tonight before you lock up," Dave added quickly. "At least ten, but as many as you can," He turned to face Jerry. "Not a bad first day for a life in show biz, eh?"

"It's not as difficult as I'd heard." Jerry said.

"Once in a lifetime," Dave grinned and took out his cell phone. "I think they're ready for prime time. Time to let the world hear your boy."

"A gig, so soon?" Jerry asked.

"Well, I'm thinking Friday anyway," he replied and sorted through numbers on his phone. "That'll give him and the boys a couple days. I know a friend who DJ's at the Viper Room who also owns the Oasis and he owes me a favor. Go and relax, I know a great barbecue place in K-Town we can hit tonight."

Jerry left the control room while Pete began to burn discs of the days work. Dave finally found the number he wanted. He heard a few rings until a voice finally answered.

"Hey Ferris!" he said. "It's Dave. Yeah… Good. Look, I've gotta call in a solid here, but you won't regret it."

At a diner on the outskirts of Las Vegas, Mr. Rader sat in a booth alone, the only patron there. It was late, but he hadn't got around to read his daily newspaper till then. A waitress passed by and refilled his coffee and he nodded silently in restrained gratitude. She left him alone again and as he took a sip, his cell phone rang.

"Rader," he answered in a low, quiet voice, making sure the waitress couldn't hear him over the diner's muzak. "Yeah. Yeah." He nodded to himself, put down his coffee and newspaper, and took out a pen from his Armani suit jacket's inside pocket. He started jotting things down on a paper napkin.

"Subject's names are Vincent Mercurio, Culver City. Jerome Spencer, same. Uh-huh. Uh-huh. At least forty-eight hours to get my people together… No sooner. No. No. I'll use only my own people. You know that's how I operate… Then do it yourself… Uh-huh. OK, fine. I'll try, but it will cost you extra… You'll hear from me as soon as I get confirmations from my people. We'll start throwing around numbers then. Right."

Mr. Rader hung up the phone and put his napkin and pen in his jacket pocket. He folded up the newspaper, left a few dollars on the table, and signaled the waitress without a word that he was finished, as he walked calmly out of the diner and into the parking lot.

Sorting through his keys, he found the one to his new, black Mercury sedan, and unlocked the driver side door, got inside, shut the door, and started the engine. He let it idle for a few seconds as he took out a cigarette from a pack in the glove compartment, lit it, and then took out his cell phone again. He dialed a number, and listened, until he heard a voice answer.

"Mr. Lockrom," he said into the phone. "It's Rader. We have an assignment."

Chapter Seven

Jerry peered over the lightly charred remains of another restrained test mouse and sunk his head, disappointed again. A veil of thin, acrid gray smoke gradually wafted out the kitchen area window. His teeth grit as he unhooked the cables from the car battery next to it on his workstation. He lifted up a clipboard with a few pages of charts and forms, rechecked his prior work before he flipped back to the top page and checked off a couple boxes with a pen. Jerry glanced around his cluttered one bedroom apartment and spotted his digital hand-held recorder. He put down his clipboard, snatched up the recorder, fiddled with its buttons for a moment, and he spoke into it.

"Wednesday, well Thursday now," he sighed and looked at his alarm clock next to his bed. "2:14 AM. I still have no idea whatsoever how the V3 formula brought Vince back from the dead. Even if I knew, that is just the beginning. His new found singing talent, his steady improvement in physical fitness, that… that *ANNOYING* new upbeat attitude!"

He paused the recorder, let out a noisy growl, paced around the apartment impatiently, and attempted to concentrate. As he looked back at the dead test mouse on his workstation, his eyes focused on it, and his pacing slowed.

"OK, OK, OK," he mumbled under his breath, scratched his head, and restarted the recorder. "This is the 34th mouse and the results are identical to the others. I've tried different concentrations and amounts of the dose, different amounts of current during electrocution, different lengths of electrocution duration, different lengths of time after electrocution before injection, and nothing. Not a goddamn thing. I'm missing something here obviously, but what? The nerve cell samples regenerate fine in vitro, but I get nothing from any living... Err... Recently living subjects."

Jerry paused the recorder again and placed it down at his workstation. Beads of cold sweat began to form on his forehead and he wiped them away with his sleeve. He put on a latex glove, released the dead mouse's restraints, picked it up by the end of its tail, walked over to his kitchen area, and lifted the lid of a step-activated garbage can. His head shook again in disappointment as he dropped its stiff little body on the pile of charred, lifeless mice inside of it. He went back to his workstation, pulled the pages from his clipboard, and was about to tear them up and toss them onto heap of mice, when he hesitated. Instead, Jerry tore them up and flushed them down his bathroom's toilet. He took off his gloves and began to record again.

"Can't have any evidence. It's getting late, but I'll continue variations until I run out of mice and take out the trash before it gets collected. Gotta get more mice in the morning too. Find a new store before this all begins to look suspect. I don't know what I'm going to do if I can't generate any results. I'm beginning to think that this has all been a bad idea, " he said while he walked over to a closet and opened it. Inside were a half dozen mice cages, though there were only a handful left in one of them. "God, I hate this part. They're so damn cute. I hope you mice don't run things in heaven or I've got some explaining to do."

Jerry switched off his recorder and put it in his back pocket. He put on his latex glove again, opened the top of the only occupied mouse cage, and took one of them out. The mouse timidly sniffed around his open palm, but didn't try to escape. Jerry brought the mouse closer to his face and spoke to it.

"Sorry, little guy," he said sadly. "If it makes you feel any better, I'd test it on the guys facing the electric chair if I could."

He carefully strapped the mouse in its tiny restraints, glanced at his alarm clock again, and wrote the time down on a new sheet of paper on the clipboard. Jerry took a deep breath and was just about to electrocute the mouse, when it looked at him with its pitch black eyes, while it struggled fruitlessly.

"Ugh. I can't do this," Jerry exhaled heavily. After he turned everything off and put the spared mouse back into its cage, he continued to talk into his recorder. "This is all wrong. All wrong. Clearly I'm missing something and I'm just too tired to think. Maybe the formula didn't bring Vince back after all. Maybe it can only work in vitro or breaks down in complex organisms. Regardless, it seems my focus has been completely hijacked by Vince and this stupid lounge act. Who knows? Maybe I'll get rich doing this instead. It'll wait. Besides, nobody else cares about us and the V3 formula anyway."

The lights of the all night taqueria a mile off the freeway in Barstow twinkled and hummed. The entire street was dark and silent except for there. Mr. Rader's black Mercury sedan pulled into its parking lot and parked. Though its engine was turned off, no one got out until a black van with tinted windows pulled in and parked along side it. Mr. Rader got out of the driver's side of the sedan and a diminutive, young man with glasses got out the passenger side. He wore a black suit similar to Mr. Rader's. Two svelte men got out of the van, who both wore similar suits, one with slick, dark hair and acne scars, the other tall and pale, with cropped blonde hair. They all approached one another and shook each other's hands.

"Mr. Lockrom," Mr. Rader turned to his short assistant. "I believe you already know Mr. Flick."

The man with the acne scars smiled slightly and nodded to them.

"This is Mr. Cunningham," Mr. Rader said pointing to the blonde man, who nodded but didn't smile. "Thank you both coming on such short notice, especially you Mr. Cunningham since you came from so far."

"No problem, sir," Mr. Cunningham replied in his proper English accent. "Especially for the kind of numbers you're talking about. Where is it?"

"It's here," Mr. Rader said and pointed to a small suitcase Mr. Lockrom held. "The last man should be arriving soon."

Mr. Flick took out a cigarette and lit it. He had only time to take a couple drags before another black sedan rolled into the parking lot, parked next to them and a tall, barrel-chested man with a crew cut stepped out.

"Is that?-" asked Mr. Lockrom.

"Uh-huh." Mr. Rader interrupted.

The hulking man approached them expressionless, simply nodding, and didn't shake any hands. Mr. Lockrom cleared his throat and tried to break the awkward silence.

"I don't believe any of you have met Mr. Strickland yet," Mr. Rader announced. "Mr. Strickland. Mr. Lockrom, Mr. Flick, and Mr. Cunningham. Follow me, gentlemen."

The men followed Mr. Rader into the taqueria, where he approached the counter and gazed up at the menu in front of an obese cashier. He hummed to himself trying to decide until Mr. Cunningham spoke softly in his ear.

"Don't you think this is slightly conspicuous?" he asked.

"Nah. I've been coming here for years," Mr. Rader replied in a calm, steady voice. "Pretty much every time I pass between LA and Vegas. What's conspicuous is that we're here at this hour and not ordering anything. Get what you want. I'm buying."

Mr. Cunningham glanced over at the menu, but gave up quickly.

"There's nothing vegetarian," he said with distain.

"And I ate an hour ago," Mr. Flick added.

"Then get something small," Mr. Rader said to Mr. Flick, and then turned his head to Mr. Cunningham. "Try the Chile Relleno then. You're not vegan too, are you?"

Mr. Cunningham narrowed his eyelids and shook his head briefly.

"Trust me on this. You won't be sorry, " Mr. Rader said.

The men ordered, waited silently inside until their food was ready, and then walked out to the patio and sat at a round, plastic table. The night air was just cool enough to show the steam as it evaporated off their food.

"Dig in and lets begin, shall we?" Mr. Rader said and immediately started to unwrap his huge burrito. The others followed suit. "Mr. Lockrom, would you please hand these men their envelopes?"

Mr. Lockrom put down his plastic fork and swallowed the mouthful he just took and opened his suitcase. One by one, he handed Flick, Cunningham, and Strickland each a large manila envelope. Mr. Strickland put his envelope on the table and began to eat. The other two opened them and examined the contents as Mr. Rader continued.

"Inside you'll find the fifty you've been promised," he said and took another bite, chewed a few times, and then went on talking with his mouth full. "The amount is two hundred and fifty upon completion, three hundred if we have it done by the end of next week." He finished chewing, swallowed, and then took another large bite.

"Inside you'll find the subject's dossiers," Mr. Lockrom said, closing his suitcase. "Not too much reading material, but all the basics. Address, numbers, work and education histories."

"Military? Government?" Mr. Flick asked. He and Mr. Cunningham pulled out and flipped through folders that they found in their envelopes. Mr. Strickland continued to eat silently.

"None," Mr. Rader swallowed, replied, and took another bite.

"No criminal record on Mr. Mercurio, not even a parking ticket. He lives with his father, Joseph Mercurio, a retired insurance executive, his mother is deceased. She had complications in childbirth," Mr. Lockrom said while he scanned over his own copy of the dossiers. "Jerry's only slightly more interesting. Also an only child, his father is a Baptist minister, very devout and he and his mother run a church outside Lawrence, Kansas. Judging by his phone and e-mail records, he doesn't really stay in touch. A couple violations for Mr. Spencer as a teenager, one count minor in possession of alcohol age fifteen, several speeding tickets, a car impounded at seventeen, and one count of malicious mayhem at eighteen. Since then, he's been clean."

"Malicious mayhem?" Mr. Cunningham asked and arched an eyebrow.

"Yes," Mr. Lockrom followed quickly and flipped the folders till he found the report. "Well, apparently, he and a group of friends had left a concert at the Hollywood Bowl quite inebriated and decided to go play around on a vacant construction site up a slope above the venue. Mr. Spencer had been horsing around on one of the sites parked tractors, when the hand brake came loose. He and his friends fell off the tractor as it rolled down the slope into the side of a parked car, a police car."

Mr. Flick and Mr. Cunningham laughed to themselves, their closed mouths full of food. Mr. Strickland kept on eating, emotionless.

"He got off easy, six months probation," Mr. Lockrom added.

Mr. Rader had already finished off his last few bites, while the others were only half way done. He took his empty plate inside, thanked the cashier, and returned.

"Mmm. I needed that. Who they are is not as important as what they know," he said. "Mr. Lockrom will continue communications and electronic surveillance on our end. Mr. Flick and Mr. Cunningham will stake out the subject's residences and gain entry as soon as they're vacant. I want all intel from the inside. Copy all computer memory. Scan any paperwork. Note anything pertaining to the V3 experiment. If we don't find what we're looking for, we shall apprehend, detain, and Mr. Strickland here will interrogate them."

"And then?" Mr. Flick asked just before he took another bite. He glanced suspiciously over at Mr. Strickland, who having just finished his food, swallowed his last bite, finally looked up and spoke.

"That will be for our employer to decide," he said in a raspy, deep voice.

"Fair enough," Mr. Cunningham said.

Chapter Eight

Dave had never heard Ferris Shirastani be quiet for so long. Ferris arrived with his friend, Ali, to hear the last take of "Sway" at the studio and both of them listened in rapturous silence. Everyone in the control room waited and grinned widely until Vince and the band finished the last note and a few seconds passed. Pete was at the mixing board again. He leaned over his console, stopped the recording, and everyone erupted in applause. Vince smiled and waved at the others through the plexiglas in the studio. Jerry nodded to him proudly and gave him a thumps up.

"How was that?" Vince asked through his microphone.

"Perfect! Just like all the others!" Pete said through the intercom.

"Great," he replied giving them an OK sign. Vince took off his large headphones, turned to the band, and shook their hands, one by one. "I think that's a wrap, boys. Excellent work tonight, stellar, really."

"Best session of my life, man," Ayman laughed.

"That's right", Kevin and Troy both said, one just a second after the next.

"Cool. Dave?" Vince said through his microphone again.

"Yeah, Vince?" Dave leaned over Pete's shoulder in the control room and spoke through the intercom.

"I'm just gonna fix my hair a bit and I'll be right up, OK?" Vince said and winked at Dave as he exited the recording room.

"Take your time," Dave replied and Pete turned off the intercom. Dave turned back to face Ferris, put his hands up, and bulged his eyes a bit. "Did I tell ya or did I tell ya?"

Ferris practically leapt into his arms as he hugged Dave with all his might, kissed him on the cheek, and erupted in laughter.

"Dave! Dave! This is it!" he cried out. "This is the big one you've always dreamed of! I mean everybody else was great, phenomenal! But this guy is like nothing on planet Earth, man!"

"So I guess this means he can play with you tomorrow?" Dave asked knowingly.

"Hell yes, dude!" Ferris said as he caught his breath a little. He turned to Ali. "I knew it. I knew it. Didn't I tell you I knew it?"

"Oh no," Ali said. "That's not what you said on the ride over."

"Nah, man. I wasn't rippin' the man or nothin'," Ferris looked back at Dave. "I mean, like swing music and all. I didn't get it, but I freakin' get it now. That kid is off the hook!"

Pete took a joint out of his metal mint box on top of the console, lit it, took a long toke, and passed it to Ferris who did the same. Still ecstatic, Ferris coughed a cloud of smoke out before offering the joint to Ali.

"Nah, man. Driving," he said and pantomimed steering a steering wheel. Ferris offered it to Jerry.

"Me too," Jerry declined.

"Oh well," Ferris said and passed it back to Pete. "Always makes me drive better." The door to the control room opened and Vince walked inside and Ferris greeted him right away and shook his hand vigorously. "Let me touch you! Let me shake this man's hand! That was insane!"

"Thanks, uhh…" Vince trailed off, a little startled by Ferris' enthusiasm.

"My name's Ferris, man!" he replied and finally stopped shaking his hand. "Also known as DJ F-Bomb. This is my homeboy, Ali."

"Cool. Right on," Vince grinned and shook Ali's hand. "So Oasis is your club, huh?"

"Well, I'm one of many owners," Ferris spoke in a comical, urbane voice. "Friday's always my night there and I'm telling everybody, I mean everybody to come on down to see music history!"

"Can we bring a couple girls?" Vince asked.

"Hell yeah!" Ferris laughed. "There's gonna be a swarm of honeys comin' down on y'all when we're done! Dave, tell me you got a copy of Vince's stuff for me. I gotta hear it again, make sure I ain't dreamin' all this!"

Pete had just inhaled another drag, but he held it, leaned over his console, picked up a jewel case with an unmarked CD in it, and handed it over to Ferris before he exhaled. Ferris clenched it in his hand triumphantly.

"Yes!" he exclaimed and patted Vince on the shoulder. "I have got to get this home to my system pronto! You and me are gonna do some wicked mash-ups, man. I got some ideas already, ya dig?"

"Sounds nice," Vince answered and smiled with gratitude.

"Sweet," he handed Vince one of his cards and exchanged a fist bump with him. "And if you ever, and I mean ever, want to come down to party central, drop by my place in Laurel Canyon, bro. Dad's out of town for months and I've got so many spare rooms, I don't know what to do with em'. We're partying tonight and every night, for real."

"Cool, thanks. Nice to meet you guys." Vince said and motioned to Jerry. "Ready to roll?"

"Hmm?" Jerry asked distracted and then snapped out of it. "Oh! Oh yeah. Cool. See you tomorrow fellas."

As soon as Jerry and Vince stepped out and started walking up the street to Jerry's car, Vince asked, "So, you bringing Lonnie?"

"Well, I hadn't really… Uhh…" Jerry hemmed and hawed.

"Come on," Vince said. "Kate's coming and you aren't going to this thing a dateless wonder."

"I dunno, man. It's just… It's kind of weird." Jerry persisted.

"Fine. Forget about it," Vince said casually, and then quickly asked. "Hey, can I barrow your phone for a sec?"

"Yeah, sure," Jerry replied without thinking, took it out of his pants pocket, and handed it over. A few seconds passed before he noticed that Vince was scrolling through his stored phone numbers. "What are you doing?"

"Hang on," Vince smiled, hit a button, and held it to his ear. Their walking slowed as Vince waited through a couple rings before someone answered. "Hey Lonnie!"

Jerry stopped cold in his tracks and feebly tried to take the phone away from Vince, but he just pivoted out of the way and kept talking. "Yeah, Hi! It's me, Vince!… Uh-huh. Look. Jerry here has something he wants to ask you."

He handed the phone back to Jerry and gleefully motioned to him to say something.

"Uhh… Hi…Uhh… Lonnie?" he spoke timidly. "Yeah… That was a great night… I just, umm… was wondering, I mean, I know it's short notice and all, but if you're not busy tomorrow night…. Ummm…Vince will be doing a show and if you want to come alo-… You do? Oh, great!… What time?"

Vince snatched the phone back from the stammering Jerry and said, "Yeah, me again. We'll be hitting din-din around sevenish and I'll be on about ten, OK? We'll give you a jingle tomorrow when we decide where we're going. That sound cool?… Excellent. See you tomorrow."

He hung up the phone, handed it back to Jerry, and began walking again. Jerry snapped out of his daze, pocketed the phone, and followed him.

"See? That wasn't so hard, now was it?" Vince asked.

At Jerry's apartment building, the black van was parked just half a block down the street. Inside, Mr. Lockrom gazed at his computers in the back and bit his fingernails occasionally. He took off the slim headset he was wearing, leaned over from his console and opened the van's driver side door. Outside stood Mr. Flick, who had an obvious look of disappointment through his dark sunglasses. In the distance

Mr. Cunningham approached the van from behind the building. Mr. Flick got in the drivers seat, took the keys out of his pants pocket, put them in the ignition, started the van, and let it idle until Mr. Cunningham caught up and got in the front passenger seat. His expression was more of disgust.

"Only a couple of bags. Nothing worth keeping, unless you enjoy barbequed mice. Next time, you're on rubbish detail," Mr. Cunningham said bitterly while he took off a pair of black rubber gloves. He tossed them out the window as the van pulled away and cruised down the street.

"Suit yourself," Mr. Flick replied. "Then you'll be the one taking all the risk. Everybody digs through the garbage in this town."

"Look, are one of you going to make the call or shall I, huh?" Mr. Lockrom asked them. They exhaled loudly, didn't respond, and just continued to look out the windows. Mr. Lockrom shook his head, put his headset back on, and punched a couple of keys on his console. After a couple seconds, he heard Mr. Rader pick up on the other end.

"Sir? Yeah, it's me," he said while he glanced over his computer screens and scrolled through the information he had, "Yeah, we don't have anything worth mentioning. Mr. Flick gained access this morning after Jerry left, searched his place from top to bottom... Yes... Yes, we were able to download everything he had there, but I see nothing interesting, unless you count his collection of celebrity nude photos... Who? ... Oh, he had a bunch, lots of Kate Winslet... No, he couldn't find anything either. Whatever he threw out must of gone out on..." He trailed off and he looked over to Mr. Cunningham.

"The morning before we got here," Mr. Cunningham said flatly.

"I doubt he'd dispose of any records pertaining to the formula here anyway," Mr. Lockrom continued. "Uh-huh... Yeah... Well, considering the equipment he has, he at least has been working on it, but like I said, we could locate none of his findings... Uh-huh... He must be keeping it elsewhere, his car, or on his person... We haven't been able to infiltrate Vince's house either. I've been monitoring the spy-cams we've placed outside there and his father still hasn't left the house. I'm beginning to doubt he ever will and if he does, he won't be going far or for very long... OK... Uh-huh... Got it. We're in route to you now. Over." He took off his headset and turned up front again. "OK. Let's return to base."

"Oh God," Mr. Flick complained. "Don't tell me we have to wait till tomorrow."

"It's worse," Mr. Lockrom went on. "You have to tail them until the show's over. It will attract too much attention if we take them beforehand."

"He's making me go to that godforsaken nightclub?", Mr. Cunningham asked, his disgust renewed.

"Tough luck," Mr. Flick chuckled quietly as he pulled the van onto the freeway.

"I'll give you earplugs, OK?" Mr. Lockrom said and turned back to his computers. "They're good ones. I used em' when I used to fire M-60s back in basic."

Almost a minute passed, as Mr. Cunningham stared out the window.

"I hate bloody nightclubs," he sneered.

Chapter Nine

The sushi restaurant Vince chose was unusually empty for a Friday night. He sat at a round table with Jerry, Lonnie, and Kate, and surveyed the many emptied sushi plates in front of him.

"Excuse me!" Vince spoke up and got the attention of his waiter, who smiled and nodded from across the restaurant. The waiter walked over and took his pen out to take his order. Vince scanned the menu one more time and said, "Uhh... let's go with one more Unagi, and guys? What are y'all game for, hmm?"

The others leaned back in their chairs, put their hands up, groaned, and shook their heads no.

"Better stop now, bubba," Jerry burped and leaned forward. "You've got a big night ahead of you and you won't want to hit that stage with a tummy ache."

"OK, just the Unagi then. Domo arigato," Vince said to the waiter, who smiled and nodded again, before he exited to the kitchen. Vince patted Jerry on the shoulder. "Manager knows best. That's why you're my main man. Somebody has to tell me what I don't want to hear from time to time, like the word 'No'."

"It's good to see you still have a healthy appetite," Lonnie laughed. "You haven't had any other symptoms since the lightning?"

"Nah. No. Not anything I can think of other than the amnesia from that day," Vince said casually. Jerry backed off into his chair slowly, trying not to look anxious. "I feel good as new! Better than ever. No trouble sleeping, no headaches, nada."

"You sure?" Kate asked.

"Actually, my eyesight has been clearer lately. Haven't worn my glasses in a while. But at this moment, I wish I had X-ray vision," Vince leered at Kate and winked playfully.

"Ha! Stop it, you perv," she laughed back at him and then gave him a quick kiss on the lips. "I don't need telepathy to know what you're thinking about."

Parked across the street outside, Mr. Flick and Mr. Lockrom sat patiently in the back of their van. Mr. Flick began to doze off, but was roused when Mr. Lockrom sat up in his chair and started to type on the keys of one of his computers.

"Mr. Rader?" Mr. Lockrom said into his headset mic. "We have a call coming into Vince's phone now. I'm patching it in." He hit a few more keys, turned up a volume knob, and turned on the internal speakers in the van so the others could hear. They waited and listened to the phone ring while Mr. Flick watched through the van's tinted windows into the restaurant across the street. He observed Vince as he broke from the conversation, took out his phone from his pants pocket, and answered it.

"Mushi Mushi! Yello!" Vince said.

"Vince? It's Dave. Where are you guys? Your band's loading in as we speak."

"It's cool, Dave. It's chill. We're finishing our last dish now. We'll be there in twenty, thirty tops. Don't wet ya' pants now. Tell the boys to get set up and run through a few numbers and I'll hop on stage the second I arrive."

"Cool. Fine. Just in case you need reminding, this is your first gig. I just want this to go smooth. Thirty tops? Promise? I'm checking my watch now, Vince. Got it?"

"Scouts honor, bub. How's the vibe there?"

"Nothing I can't handle, but Ayman's bitchin' a little. Insists on setting up his own equipment. These jazz bassist guys, you know. They treat their gear like Ferraris. They're worse than heavy metal drummers."

"No doubt. See ya' soon. Oh good here's the Unagi!" Vince said and hung up his phone.

Mr. Lockrom and Mr. Flick both nodded to each other and checked their wristwatches.

When the show at the Oasis was just wrapping up, Mr. Cunningham took the earplugs out of his ears and put back in his communications earpiece. He cleared his throat and slowly started to make his way through the exuberant crowd as they exited the club.

"Well, that took long enough... Thanks for the earplugs, Lockrom. Couldn't hear a thing," he mumbled into the mic hidden in his right lapel and kept his head down.

"You're telling me that you didn't listen to any of that show?" Mr. Rader asked through his headset.

"No," he replied blandly.

"You should have heard at least a little. This kid's got some real talent," Mr. Rader said. "I guess this proves that whatever they did with the V3 works."

"I really don't care. It's just another job." he said.

"Jeez', Cunningham. What the hell do you do for fun?" Mr. Flick joined them on the headsets.

"I run," he responded while rummaging through his coat pocket until he found his fake backstage pass. "And when I do, I do it alone and someplace quiet."

Mr. Cunningham looked through the entrance to the backstage and could see Vince surrounded by Dave, Kate, Jerry, and Lonnie as they hugged and congratulated him. While he waited for his turn to pass, he spoke once more to his colleagues outside in the van.

"I'm passing through now. Be ready at the back door when they move. Copy?" he said.

"Understood. Motor's running and we're standing by. Just tell him Mr. Shirastani has arranged transport to the after party like we rehearsed, and then we'll do the rest," Mr. Rader replied.

Mr. Cunningham showed his pass at the security guard at the stage's barricade, who was already distracted by a group of love struck women as they begged desperately to get backstage. He glanced at his pass for a second and waived him through. Mr. Cunningham passed by the side of the stage and was only a few steps away from the backstage entrance when Ayman erupted in an argument with one of the club's stagehands.

"This is my rig!" Ayman insisted, trying to pull his bass head away from the stagehand. "I told you at the load in! Only I touch my gear!"

"This is our club! We move the gear here!" the stagehand shouted back and recoiled away. As Ayman's hands slipped off, the stagehand lost his balance and the bass head came loose from his arms. The commotion above Mr. Cunningham drew his attention for a split second and he turned slightly to face the stage. The bass rig fell like a stone and its bottom corner impacted precisely on top of Mr. Cunningham's left foot where it met the ankle. A dull thud and an immediate eerie crunching sound were followed by an ear splitting scream from Mr. Cunningham.

Everybody in the van outside were completely startled, leapt in their seats almost a foot each, and ripped the squealing overloaded earpieces from their ears. Inside, Kevin, Troy, and a handful of security guards rushed the stage and tried to break up the scuffle that had begun between Ayman and the stagehand.

"That was your fault!" the stagehand yelled.

"No way! If you hadn't touched my gear, none of this would have happened!" he yelled back.

Ferris joined Dave and the others backstage and beckoned them away from the commotion.

"Don't worry. This is my place. I'll handle it. You guys take off," Ferris reassured them.

"He's right," Dave agreed straight away as they started to make their way to the rear exit of the club. "Believe me. The farther you are away when stuff like this occurs, the better."

At the side of the stage, Mr. Cunningham clenched his jaw, breathed heavily, and struggled to endure the intense waves of pain he was feeling in his ankle. He ignored the crowd above him asking if he was OK and if they could help. Mr. Rader finally put on his earpiece again and spoke to him.

"Mr. Cunningham?!" Mr. Rader pleaded. "Come in! Talk to me! What happened? What's your status? Over!"

"It's my ankle!" he grunted. "I need medical assistance, you bastard!"

"I'm so sorry, sir," Ferris dashed out from the backstage entrance, thinking that Mr. Cunningham was talking to him and not to the others in the van. "I'll call an ambulance right away! I hope we can settle this accident without any legal complications, right?"

Ferris pulled out his cell phone and started to dial, but Mr. Cunningham hopped up on his good right ankle and put his hand over it, which stopped Ferris from dialing.

"*NO!*" Mr. Cunningham blurted. He then lowered his voice, and tried desperately to block out the pain. "I'm, uhh, actually in the country illegally," He spoke up making sure that Mr. Rader knew he was speaking to him as well. "My friends are outside waiting to pick me up. If you just help my... Umm... Hop out to them, I'll get taken care of. I promise."

"You sure?" Ferris asked while he helped him stay up on one foot.

"Positive," He replied. "Just get me to the front and you'll never see me again. I swear."

"Well, OK," Ferris reluctantly agreed. Mr. Cunningham leaned on him as Ferris helped him hop his way to the front entrance of the club.

"Thanks for understanding," Mr. Cunningham winced.

Behind them, the stagehand had been pulled away kicking and screaming by the security guards, while Kevin and Troy comforted Ayman who knelt over his bass head on the ground and inspected it for damage.

"Oh no. Oh baby," Ayman looked over his bass head and feared the worst. "Papa's here. Papa's going to make you all better."

Outside the club, Mr. Flick drove the van up to the front entrance just as Ferris and Mr. Cunningham made it through the front doors. He leapt out, opened the van's sliding side door, and took over for Ferris. As he helped Mr. Cunningham into the van, Ferris was a little bewildered by the high tech gear in the van and how fast they moved. He barely had just enough time to take out one of his business cards and offer it to them.

"No! No, thank you!" Mr. Rader smiled and waved him away. Mr. Lockrom helped Mr. Cunningham into one of the vans chairs and Mr. Flick got back in the drivers seat. "We're fine!"

"Are you su-?" Ferris said as Mr. Rader slammed the side door shut and the van peeled out of the parking lot. Puzzled, Ferris watched them drive out of sight while he still held out his business card.

Mr. Cunningham started to bellow and breathe heavily while they drove away.

"God damn it!" he yelled as he clutched his left ankle. "I can't bloody believe this! What the hell?!"

"Oh, this is just perfect," Mr. Flick said from the driver's seat. "Now what?"

"We abort," Mr. Rader said.

"Again?!" Mr. Lockrom asked angrily.

"We're a man down. He's too much baggage. We've lost the element of surprise," Mr. Rader replied. "We take him back to base and Mr. Strickland will patch him up."

"Strickland?" Mr. Lockrom asked.

"He can fix bones just as easily as he can break them. Trust me, I know," Mr. Rader said. "Tomorrow, we three take Jerry at his place and Mr. Strickland will go to Vince's, wait till he comes home, and take him there. We'll regroup and take both of them to the boss. Got it?"

"What about Vince's dad?" Mr. Flick asked.

"Mr. Strickland can handle him," Mr. Rader said.

Chapter Ten

The sun rose while Jerry parked his car on a street behind his apartment building. He was groggy, but still smiled as he savored the memory of the night of passion that he spent with Lonnie. As he turned to stroll down the long alley on the side of his building to get to the front, the black van pulled out slowly and silently behind him and then stopped. Jerry was too sleepy to notice, but did hear the noise of an overweight bum near the other end of the alley as he rummaged through his building's recycling bins. Mr. Flick glanced from around a corner, caught sight of Jerry, and slipped back again.

"Target in sight," Mr. Flick said into his lapel mic and started to calmly stroll into the alley. "I'm closing in."

"As soon as he's down, we move. Move fast," Mr. Rader said through his earpiece. "We have him cut off at this end. Remember, that gun only has three shots before you have to reload, so make them count."

"I got this," he replied.

The bum stopped rummaging for a moment as Jerry approached, smiled, and extended his filthy hand.

"Hey buddy. You got eighty-five cents?" the bum asked in a slurred, gravely drawl.

"Sorry dude." Jerry put his hands up.

But just as he was just passed the bum, he saw Mr. Flick reach into his coat pocket, pull out a long-barreled tranquilizer pistol, and began to aim it at him. Without thinking, Jerry grabbed the bum by his shoulders and jerked him aside, and took cover behind him, just a split second before Mr. Flick could get off a shot. The dart hit dead center between the bum's shoulder blades, which caused him to flinch abruptly, and then quickly go limp into Jerry's arms.

"Sorry, dude," Jerry said, face to face with the bum.

"Oh, that's alright," the bum said with a delirious grin, just before he slipped into complete unconsciousness.

Mr. Flick had to re-cock his pistol to load in another dart, but it didn't reload on his first attempt, which made him growl. Once he got it loaded correctly the second time, he aimed again. But before he could get off the second shot, Jerry lurched forward and hurled the full weight of the limp body of the bum on top of him. The collision caused Mr. Flick's pistol to slip out of his hands and it went off the moment it hit the ground. The dart barely missed Jerry's head, whizzed down the alley, and landed in the front left tire of the van. Though the dart punctured the rubber of the tire, it didn't pop it. It remained stuck. Its rear half protruded out as it began a slow air leak.

Jerry bolted while Mr. Flick struggled to get the heavy, sleeping, smelly heap off of his skinny body. The van took off at the other end of the alley and began their pursuit. Jerry had made it halfway down another street behind a strip mall when he saw Mr. Flick turned the corner behind him. Jerry quickly lost ground as the lean Mr. Flick sprinted closer. The van caught up and came to a screeching halt at the end of the street, which cut him off. Jerry stopped, almost out of breath, and started to dart his head around.

He saw a row of back doors behind the strip mall and tried frantically to open them one at a time, but the first two were locked. By the time he made it to his third try, Mr. Flick came within ten feet of him, stopped, and aimed his tranquilizer gun at him again. Luckily, the third door was unlocked, so Jerry threw it open and dashed inside. Mr. Flick roared in frustration, abandoned his shot, and continued to chase him.

"Help! Help! He's got a gun!" Jerry screamed blindly. Not having paid attention to the group of men inside the building's main room, he bolted through, burst through the room's front door, and ran outside across the adjacent street.

Mr. Flick made it two steps inside the main room and stopped in his tracks having seen that he was now confronted with a group of a dozen sweaty, muscle bound men in wrestling gear. He pointed his tranquilizer gun at them and waved it back and forth, in an effort to cover all of them.

"Stay back!" Mr. Flick shouted and looked up for a split second to see the words 'BRAZILLIAN JU-JITSU" painted on the wall in large capital letters. He flinched just enough to accidentally pull the trigger and his last dart shot off into the shoulder of the class' Instructor.

"Take him," the Instructor said and pointed his finger at Mr. Flick just before he slipped into unconsciousness. Mr. Flick gasped and tried to run out the back door again, but was pulled back by the sea of angry wrestlers.

Jerry ran as fast as he could. His heart pounded faster than he ever felt before. He doubled back to where he parked his car, darted his head around as he ran, and looked to see if any one was still chasing him. Though he hadn't seen anybody, Jerry didn't slow down until he was only a few steps from his car. His hands trembled violently as he pulled out his keychain and managed to unlock his car door. He started the ignition just as the van careened around the corner behind him.

"*AHH*!!!" Jerry yelled when he saw it in his rear view mirror.

He stomped on the accelerator, peeled out of his parking space, and raced down the street. The van had caught up to within twenty feet of his car by the time he matched the van's speed. Beads of ice cold sweat poured down Jerry's panic stricken face. He saw a red light at the intersection ahead, and his panic deepened when he saw oncoming traffic to his right. So he pulled hard on the steering wheel, making a sharp right. His car nearly flipped over, briefly rising onto its two left wheels, before coming back down to the ground again after he completed the turn. The oncoming traffic managed to come to screeching halts and fanned out all over the intersection as they tried not to get hit.

Mr. Rader saw a clear path through the cars and tried to make the same turn, but the pressure from the dart's puncture on the front left tire finally caused it to blow completely. Mr. Lockrom let out a high-pitched shriek and braced himself as Mr. Rader struggled desperately to hold on to the steering wheel of his out of control van. Mr. Rader managed to keep it from flipping over. It didn't hit any cars, but he could not stop or steer enough to avoid a fire hydrant, which they were in a collision course.

Both Mr. Rader and Mr. Lockrom screamed as the van jumped the intersection's curb and smashed into the fire hydrant. Mr. Rader's driver side airbag instantly went off and pinned him in his seat. The collision broke the hydrant off the concrete, ruptured the whole front end of the van, and spewed a geyser of water into the vans interior. Within seconds, the inside of the van had almost filled with water from top to bottom. Mr. Rader managed to get off a couple shots from his pistol. One popped the airbag, the other shattered the driver's side window.

Mr. Rader managed to finally get his door open and he was immediately vaulted out of the van behind a gush of cold whitewater. He hit the concrete sidewalk hard. Dazed, he staggered over to the vans side door and opened it, which let loose the water from inside. Mr. Lockrom flew out and hit the ground just as he did, convulsed from the short-circuiting machines, while he still held onto one of his laptops. Mr. Rader helped him to his feet. Both coughed violently while they tried to get the water out of their lungs and sinuses. Mr. Rader gazed around at about a half dozen people in the intersection, who got out of their stopped cars and gawked in amazement.

"We've got to get out here! Run!" he shouted into Mr. Lockrom's ear. He tried to pull him away, but Mr. Lockrom, who still twitched from being electrocuted, struggled at first to get back into the van.

"But the gear! The gear!" he insisted. Both of them looked inside and saw the remainder of Mr. Lockrom's computers and monitors as they violently hissed and sparked.

"Forget it! It's gone! We've got to move now!" Mr. Rader yanked him with all his strength away and shoved him forward as they both began to sprint back down the street where they came from. "We've got to find Mr. Flick!"

"Well, maybe we can still salvage this one!" Mr. Lockrom shouted deliriously and held up the one laptop he managed to save as they ran.

"Damn it!" Mr. Rader shouted angrily to himself.

The crowd of onlookers started to take pictures of the van's watery wreckage, and paid hardly any attention to Mr. Rader and Mr. Lockrom as they ran out of sight around another street corner. While he coughed up water and gasped for breath, Mr. Rader scanned his surroundings and grabbed Mr. Lockrom by his shoulders to slow him down.

"Ease down. Ease down. We're clear," Mr. Rader said to him eventually and acclimated into a steady, but measured voice. They both could hear the sirens of police and emergency vehicles approach the crash site behind them. "Walk. Don't run, don't give anyone eye contact."

"What are we going to do?" Mr. Lockrom asked as he slowed to a steady walking pace along side him.

"I don't know. Wait," he replied and fished through his pockets for his cell phone. His pants were still soaked and he shook the water from his phone. Before he could touch it, Mr. Lockrom grabbed his arm and stopped him.

"Don't!" he interjected and then lowered his voice as they walked. "It has to dry out before you power it on again or you'll ruin it."

Frustrated, Mr. Rader almost turned it on anyway, but clenched his jaw, took a deep breath, and put it back into his pocket. They walked another block before he spoke again.

"We have to find Mr. Flick," he said and pointed down the street. "Last I saw them was another block that way and to the left."

Mr. Lockrom nodded and they continued to march down the street. They both went pale with fear as they heard more sirens approach from behind them. Mr. Rader grabbed Mr. Lockrom's arm before he could turn around to look.

"Don't. Just keep walking. Slower now." Mr. Rader let go of his arm. They both slowed their pace to a casual stroll as they saw an ambulance and a half dozen police cars whiz past them and turn the left corner where they headed.

"You don't think?..." Mr. Lockrom asked.

"Don't know. We have to see," he replied.

The two made the left corner to see those vehicles joining another ambulance and two police cars already in front to the Brazilian Ju-jitsu Fitness Center. They passed the scene on the opposite side of the street and could see the Instructor being revived by paramedics with smelling salts, while his students hovered around them.

"Where is- Oh my God," Mr. Lockrom said, but quickly looked straight forward, having glimpsed more paramedics taking out a body with a blanket, covered by everything but Mr. Flick's shoes, out of the Fitness Center.

"He's gone. Keep walking. Don't look." Mr. Rader caught a glimpse too and snapped his head forward. They waited until they were another block away until they started walking faster.

"But... But how? How could this happen?" Mr. Lockrom asked intensely.

"Shut up. I'm trying to think," Mr. Rader said back sharply. A few seconds later, he spoke again. "OK. OK. First, we have to find a pay phone. We have to get to Mr. Strickland and regroup."

"A pay phone? What pay phone?!", Mr. Lockrom scoffed. "There's no such thing as a pay phone anymore!"

"Then we have to get to Vince's and hope Mr. Strickland is still there," he replied.

As he panted heavily, Jerry tried to control his shock. He gradually slowed his car down enough to not look suspicious. His eyes quickly checked his rear view mirrors and the road as he fumbled through his coat until he found his cell phone. He had trouble dialing at first with his trembling hands and had to start over after his first attempt.

"Damn!" he cursed. He steadied himself getting the number right and listened intensely as it began to ring. "C'mon, Vince. Pick up, man. Pick up."

Jerry let out a primal yell as Vince's voice mail message came up instead. He hung up and redialed, but it happened again. He put the cell phone down on the passenger seat and hit his dashboard twice as hard as he could with his right fist in frustration. It hurt, but he was still too high on adrenaline to feel it. Behind a row of cars, he stopped at a stoplight and waited impatiently for it to turn green.

"What am I going to do? What am I going to do?" he jabbered quickly under his breath. "I… I… I can't go to the police. I can't explain this. I can't go home. I can't go home. Who the hell were those guys? How could they have known about the formula?"

The light changed and he took off again. Jerry continued to talk to himself until he made it to Vince's house. Though he made sure to park around the corner, Jerry walked just shy of the point of running until he made it to Vince's front lawn. He looked around nervously, but couldn't see or hear anything out of the ordinary.

"Oh God," he muttered and hid behind a large bush. "Where is he? His car's not here."

He dialed Vince's number again on his cell phone and waited this time until Vince's voicemail message finished.

"Vince!" he shouted into the phone, and then piped down to a forceful whisper. "Vince. Pick up, man. I'm in trouble. I think we're in trouble.

Call me. For God's sake call me. Don't come home. You're in da-"
Jerry nearly dropped his phone when he saw Vince stroll down the
sidewalk in front of him and sip from a coffee in a to go cup. Having
juggled his phone frantically for a second or two before getting a firm
grasp on it, he hung up, and put it in his pocket again. He pounced out
of the bushes and grabbed Vince by his arm as he passed him.

"Whoa! Easy there, tiger!" Vince chuckled, despite being a little bit
startled. He yanked his arm from Jerry's grasp and put his hands up and
tried not to spill his coffee. "What are doing in there?"

"Vince!" Jerry said in his raspy, forced whisper. "Get in here. Now!"

"No," he backed up a step and looked around, obviously puzzled.
"You come out here. I've had about enough of your fun and games, mister."

"Why didn't you answer your phone?", Jerry asked.

"I was too busy making sweet, sweet lo-o-o-ove," he sang the words
loudly with a giant grin and then spoke normally again. "I turned it off.
I didn't want any interruptions."

"We've got to get out of here," Jerry said and peeked his head out
like a frightened rabbit. "These… These guys are after me and I think
they're after you too."

"Guys?" Vince asked looking around some more and took another
sip from his coffee. "What guys? What kind of guys? Why would they be
after us for? What, I've got fans that are stalking me already? That was
quick."

"What? No!" Jerry struggled for words.

"The Paparazzi? Jesus, you'd think they got enough pictures of me
last night," Vince said, turned away from him, and started to walk towards his front door.

"No! Vince! Don't!" Jerry pleaded and grabbed his shoulder trying
to hold him back. Vince shook him off again and turned back to him.

"Stop it, Jer'," Vince said and grew frustrated. "Just tell me what
happened, OK?"

"OK…. Uhh…" Jerry tried to come up with the right words. "I… Uhh… Was coming home this morning from Lonnie's just before-"

"Hey! Alright!" Vince interrupted and gave him a chug on his shoulder. "You finally scored with Lonnie! I knew you had it in you, big guy."

"No, Vince… I… These guys in suits tried to abduct me!" Jerry grew weaker as he spoke. "They might be after you too."

"OK, OK fine," Vince said while he attempted to reassure him and started to walk towards his front door again. "Let's go inside and we'll talk it over, OK?"

"No! No!" Jerry pleaded "You can't go in there. They might be after your dad too."

"My dad?" Vince laughed as he looked through his keychain for the front door key. "What for? Did the guys from Jeopardy finally get tired of him yelling at the TV? C'mon, the man's harmless."

Vince opened the front door and entered and Jerry reluctantly followed. Just as Jerry shut the door behind them they both threw their hands up and shouted, "*WHOA*!!" as Mr. Mercurio whipped around only a few feet from them with a pistol in his hand and pointed it at them. The cup of coffee slipped out of Vince's hand and fell on the floor behind him, which caused its plastic lid to pop off and spill its remains.

"Damn it!" Mr. Mercurio shouted while he put the pistol's safety on and thrust it into his pants pocket. Vince and Jerry were horrified to see that Mr. Mercurio was in the process of dragging Mr. Strickland's dead body to the garage, wrapped in black garbage bags.

"Dad! What the hell?! Is that man dead?! Did you kill him?!" Vince ranted.

"Oh my God! Oh my God! Oh my God!" Jerry jabbered at the same time.

"Shut up! Shut up! Now! The both of you!" Mr. Mercurio shouted back, until they stopped. Stunned, Jerry and Vince stood still for a moment and concentrated on their breathing so they wouldn't faint, and Mr. Mercurio continued. "Vince! Get his ankles! The trunk's open in the garage! We've got to get out of here! Move! Now!"

"OK, OK, OK, OK," Vince muttered nervously to himself as he helped his father carry the lifeless body to the garage.

"What happened?! Who is this guy?!" Jerry demanded.

"Keep it down!" Mr. Mercurio scolded him in a loud whisper as he and Vince heaved Mr. Strickland's body into the trunk of his car and shut it. "You both can't be part of this."

"Part of what?" Out of breath, Vince asked while he quickly wiped the sweat from his brow.

"Get in the car, son," he ordered Vince and then pointed at Jerry. "Where's your car?"

"Uhh. Just around the block," Jerry stammered.

"Good! Get it and follow me. We're going to the end of Lucile Street, by the river. You know where, right?" Mr. Mercurio asked.

"Yeah, yeah," Jerry replied and thought aloud. "That's where Vince and I used to smoke-"

Jerry instantly froze, his eyes bugged out, and he cut off his words with a hiccup. Vince hung his head for a moment just before getting in the car's passenger seat. Mr. Mercurio gave him a stern look before he got in himself, then rolled down the window and spoke to Jerry, but didn't look at him.

"Get your car. Now. Meet us there. Go now," he said blankly and then opened the garage door with a remote. Jerry was about to bolt out when he barked at him, "Walk! Don't run!"

Jerry nearly tripped on his feet as he slowed down and proceeded out of the garage with a steady march. Mr. Mercurio's old Cadillac gently pulled out of the driveway and the garage door shut behind them. Vince stared straight ahead for a few seconds until his father finally looked back at him and broke the silence.

"After all this time, I didn't think they'd catch up to me," Mr.

Mercurio said grimly and turned his eyes back on the road. "Bastard tried to get me in my own kitchen. I guess they forgot how handy I was with a cleaver."

"Dad, I...." Vince struggled for his words.

"Just let me finish. I've got to get this out all at once or I just can't do it," Mr. Mercurio went on. "Your last name really isn't Mercurio. It's Bellici. We've been in the Witness Protection Program since you were a baby. My name is really Vince and you're Vince, Jr."

"Mom? Is she? I mean, was she?..." Vince asked gravely.

"She is gone, son. It wasn't in childbirth," he replied and struggled to hold back tears. "They... These men... Men I thought I trusted, gunned us down while she was eight months pregnant with you. It left her brain-dead, but they were able to save you. I was in a coma for three months. That scar on my belly isn't from my appendectomy and the one on the side of my head isn't from a machine shop accident. I'm... I'm sorry, son. I can't tell you anymore now, not till I know what our next move is."

"Wha... Wha..." Vince trailed off as he tried to absorb it all. "But they tried to get to Jerry too."

"Jerry?" Mr. Mercurio paused. "Why him?"

"I don't know. Maybe they were trying to get to me and couldn't find me, so they wanted to get to him first," Vince said.

"Are you sure?" he asked as he pulled the car onto the freeway. "It's possible. But this guy doesn't look like the kind I was used to. Maybe they wanted to hold you for ransom too because of your new... Profession. I hope you understand now, son. It wasn't that I didn't want you to know the truth. It's just... If you became famous, my old enemies might find me again and you'd be in danger too."

"So... Uncle Rolf?" Vince asked.

"Rolf's been my case officer from the beginning," Mr. Mercurio replied. "Of course, we're not the only people he watches over. He's been a real friend to both of us, but he cannot know you and Jerry are wrapped up in all of this. I've got to be sure both of you are in the clear before we do anything else. Trust me on this. I'm ashamed to say I've done this before. We'll dump the big guy in the trunk, you and Jerry stay out of sight for a few days, and I'll go to Uncle-" He stopped and corrected himself. "I'll go to Rolf and find out who's after us. Damn."

"What do you think Jerry and I should do?" Vince asked as they pulled off the freeway.

"Get out of town, but not too far," he replied, pulled out his wallet, and handed all the cash he had to Vince. "Take this. Stay off the grid. No phone calls, no credit cards. Get to an ATM and both of you take out as much as you can, but don't go to another one again until I call you. These guys are serious. Understand?"

"Yeah, yeah," Vince answered and quickly nodded his head. His father glanced over at him as they pulled down the end of Lucile Street. He could see the totality of the situation beginning to weigh down on his son. Mr. Mercurio turned the car around and backed up to the guardrail overlooking the embankment to Ballona Creek. He paused and put his hand on his son's shoulder. "Look, I'm sorry during all these years that I was so protective. I only wanted you to be safe. I was just trying to protect you from all this. I'll make things right again. I promise."

Vince nodded as his father parked and stopped the engine. They waited for a moment until Jerry's car pulled into the street and parked on the corner about fifty feet in front of them. They both got out and Mr. Mercurio pointed to the trunk.

"Open it and wait for me," he said and walked over to Jerry's car. Jerry rolled the window down, still traumatized. "Stay calm, kid. Keep your eyes peeled and honk if you see anybody pulling in. You got me?"

Jerry nodded and surveyed the area discreetly. Mr. Mercurio walked briskly as he returned to his car. Vince got out and helped pick Mr. Strickland's massive, plastic wrapped body out of the trunk, and heaved it over the guardrail. They both grunted and stretched their backs while it slid halfway down the embankment.

"You and Jerry get going," Mr. Mercurio ordered him. "I'll tip the cops off and then I'll call you by Monday at the latest to let you know what I've found out." He hugged him tightly. "I love you. Be safe."

"I love you too, Dad," Vince said and held on until his dad released him. Mr. Mercurio quickly got back into his car and sped off. Vince got in the passenger seat of Jerry's car and they took off in the opposite direction.

"Oh my God. Oh my God. Your dad, he… He just murdered a man, for Christ's sake!" Jerry babbled nervously. "What the hell happened? Where are we going to go?"

"Let me think for a second," Vince said. After a moment, Vince fumbled through his wallet and pulled out a business card. "I have an idea. I'll tell you about it on the way."

Chapter Eleven

"Look, man. I don't know if this is such a good idea," Jerry said as they parked the car in front of a tall, cast iron electric gate. "Do we even have the right place?"

"This has to be it," Vince insisted, hopped out of the car, and walked over to an intercom station embedded in the red brick wall next to the gate. "This is a private road. There's no other place anywhere near here. This has to be it."

Jerry rolled his window down, but didn't get out and kept the engine running. While he tried to repress his panic, Jerry glanced in his rear view mirror and into the sides of the heavily wooded road of deepest, darkest Laurel Canyon. He leaned out his window and was about to speak when Vince interrupted him.

"Just let me do the talking and try to stay calm, OK?" Vince reassured him. After a couple seconds, Jerry nodded in agreement. Vince pressed the intercom call button, which made an annoying buzzing noise. After a couple seconds, a voice answered.

"What's up? Who is it?" the voice responded. Vince knew it was Ali.

"Hey there! It's Vince! This where the party's at?" Vince asked loudly and laughed.

"Quit screwing around out there, guys! Bring up the new keg. This one's nearly dry," he responded impatiently.

"No, Ali. Really! It's me! I'm here with Jerry," Vince said.

"Wait! Look up for a sec, up at the camera," Ali said. Jerry leaned out of the car window and looked upwards and waved with Vince at the surveillance camera on top of the brick wall. Ali burst back on the intercom, but his voice was so loud that it distorted the speaker. "No way! I can't believe it! It's really you!"

Vince looked back at Jerry and winked, giving him an OK symbol with one of his hands. They could hear Ali shouting in Farsi, followed by the sound of cheers in the background.

"Get up here, man!" Ali shouted joyfully and a buzzer rang. The huge electronic gate unlocked and swung open mechanically. Vince got back into the car and they started to drive up the long driveway and the gates slowly closed behind them as they passed.

"See, everything's going to be fine. Just let me continue to do the talking, OK?" Vince said. They both gasped in awe as they approached Ferris' gigantic Hacienda style mansion complex. "My god, this guy's loaded. We've got to call the girls up here."

"What? No way!" Jerry snapped back. "Your dad told us to lay low."

"Well, don't you think the guys who are after us will be after them?" Vince asked. The question stunned Jerry for a moment and made him struggle for an answer, but he finally came up with one.

"Look, Kate's a news reporter and Lonnie's a billionaire's daughter," Jerry responded. "They're the last people those goons would mess with if they don't want to attract attention. We can't see them until all this gets sorted. It's too dangerous."

"Dangerous? Look at the security in this place!" Vince said.

"Forget it! It's not worth it. They know that we'd try to reach them somehow. They would be expecting that," Jerry replied. "I'm your manager, remember? You have to trust me on this."

"OK, OK, OK! Whatever," Vince said as they pulled up to the growing crowd of revelers in front of them. "There's Ferris. Be cool."

"I know! I know," Jerry said as he slowed the car down to park. "Let you do the talking. Right."

They stopped the car, got out, and were instantly greeted with cheers, pats on the back from the men, hugs and kisses from the women, most dressed in swimwear. Ferris edged his way past his friends to embrace Vince.

"You're here! You made it!" Ferris laughed.

"Hey, thanks for having us!" Vince replied. "I was worried we'd be arriving a little early for the party tonight."

"Tonight?! Ha! This one's been going on since last night!" Ferris shouted to the crowd. They cheered, raised their red plastic cups, and drank from them. He put his arm around Vince's shoulder and beckoned the crowd inside the complex's main atrium. "Come on! Come on in. Let me show you around. Just leave your car there. From here on out, Brother Ferris is gonna take care of y'all."

The crowd walked through a massive hallway decorated with modern art paintings and sculptures. The backyard had an enormous pool area populated by dozens of other partiers who swam, drank, played volleyball, and bathed in the sun. A DJ was spinning drum and bass records under a portable canopy and a handful of girls in bikinis were dancing.

"Check it, bro." Ferris pointed out to the crowd. "What's mine is yours, understand? Take it from me, just snap your fingers and any of those fly honeys are yours, eh?"

"Oooo, thanks. But I just had one last night and I think she's a keeper," Vince replied.

"Suit yourself. More for me then," Ferris said and introduced Vince to a group of friends by the poolside. "Hey y'all! You remember this guy?"

They all waved and said hello, some raising their cups to toast him. Ferris led Vince and Jerry to the poolside bar made with red brick and ornamented tiles, and went behind it.

"What's your poison? Vodka martini?" Ferris asked.

"Yeah, sure." Vince smiled and turned to Jerry.

"Umm, cool. Sounds good," Jerry said.

"I do have one favor, though," Vince mentioned to Ferris while he started to mix their drinks.

"Sure. Name it," Ferris replied instantly.

"Can we crash here for the weekend?" Vince asked casually. "There's been an army of paparazzi camped outside our places ever since that show and we thought we'd lay low for the weekend."

"Can you?!" Ferris responded, clearly overjoyed. "Man, this is my dream come true! Hell yes! Stay all month!"

"Oh that's OK. We don't want to be a burden," Jerry said. "We barely got away-"

"Away from those press vultures, that is!" Vince interrupted. "We couldn't even pack any clothes."

"A burden, this guy says!" Ferris laughed as he shook the martini shaker. "You guys will be treated like kings! Gods! Vince, I'm giving you my dad's room. He's about your build. Take any of his suits you want. You too, Jerry. I'll give you the room next door."

"Won't your dad be pissed?" Vince asked.

"What? Nah!" Ferris grinned as he poured them two martinis. "He's out of town, gone for weeks at least, months, probably. Most of those suits up there, he's never even worn. Hell, he'd never even know if they were gone. Here. Drink up, boys. You have some catching up here to do, eh?"

They raised their glasses and all took long swigs. Vince grinned and smacked his lips a little.

"Thanks, Ferris. We owe you one," he said.

"No trouble, man," Ferris patted them both one at a time on the shoulder from across the bar. "I should be thanking you. Now it's real party. We got crazy security here, homies, and more guns than a Schwarzenegger movie. None of those TMZ guys will bug you here."

After the sun went down, Mr. Rader and Mr. Lockrom finally made it to the Mercurio's house. It took them hours to get there by bus. Their guns were drawn, while they silently crept through the open front door and searched the house, but it was empty.

"Mr. Lockrom? Down here," Mr. Rader said from the kitchen, holstered his pistol and looked grim.

"The hidden cameras we set up are still here. His car's still out front. Where the hell is he? You find anything?" he asked, creeped down the stairs cautiously, joined him in the kitchen, and holstered his pistol as well. Mr. Rader switched on a light above the kitchen sink and pointed out a bit of dried blood on the floor.

"They missed a spot," he said blankly.

"What?!" Mr. Lockrom stumbled back a step in amazement. "They got Strickland too? That's impossible!" He started to pace around while Mr. Rader stood motionless. "I can't believe this! This is stupid! We were safer working with the Company! That's it. I give up."

"Twenty-one years," Mr. Rader said.

"What?" he asked.

"Twenty-one years, I knew Jason Strickland," Mr. Rader went on as his melancholy turned to determination. "We were in the Gulf together. That man saved my life more than once and there's no way we're quitting now."

"But we can't-" Mr. Lockrom said, but was interrupted.

"No way!" Mr. Rader's tone of voice turned sour, but he would not look at him. He continued to stare at the drop of dried blood on the floor. "We still have until Monday."

"But I won't have my system back up until at least then," Mr. Lockrom said at the verge of throwing a tantrum. "It took me ages to get that system together!"

"Here." Mr. Rader took out his keychain and took one of the keys off its ring. "Take Strickland's car and go out and find a Radio Shack or something."

"This late? Where?" Mr. Lockrom asked, totally exasperated.

"I don't care! Get moving!" he replied angrily, glared, and pointed his finger at him. His outburst made Mr. Lockrom stop his pacing.

"Let me think," Mr. Lockrom sighed heavily and thought to himself for a moment. "If I find some gear good enough tonight, I might have some surveillance, at least our phone taps back up and running by tomorrow night."

"Good," Mr. Rader replied quietly again and stared back at the bloodstain. Mr. Lockrom nodded silently and backed out of the kitchen, and then out the front door. Mr. Rader remained still, closed his eyes, and bowed his head.

The sun was setting just as Mr. Mercurio's car pulled into Uncle Rolf's driveway in Modesto. Dressed in his bathrobe and slippers, Uncle Rolf opened both his front and screen door before Mr. Mercurio got out, approached him, and spoke before he shut off his engine.

"C'mon. C'mon. Get in here, will ya?" Uncle Rolf said and scratched the thinning grey hair on his head. He lifted his reading glasses and peered out in the distance to make sure that nobody had spotted them as Mr. Mercurio got out of his car. "Jesus, that message you left on my machine scared the hell out of me. Seriously man, are you tripping out or something? Maybe you're having a stroke."

Mr. Mercurio walked inside Uncle Rolf's house with him, kept his head down, though his eyes darted about. He waited until the front door was shut before he raised his head. Without a word said, he quickly moved to shut all the curtains in the front of the house and turned off all the lights.

"Poppa Vinnie? Pop? What the hell, man?" Uncle Rolf stood still and watched Mr. Mercurio as he paced around the house for a few seconds and mumbled to himself under his breath. "Look man, your message didn't make a whole lot of sense, but I did what you asked anyway."

Mr. Mercurio finally sat down on one of Uncle Rolf's sofas and motioned him to sit down next to him in an easy chair. He took a deep breath, closed his eyes for a moment, and then leaned forward towards Uncle Rolf. He waited for him to sit before he spoke.

"OK. First tell me everything you know about the stiff," **Mr.** Mercurio said plainly.

"Well, I can't tell you much, Pop," Uncle Rolf said right away. "I mean, not any more than I think you know already. Like you said, this guy looked like a griller, not a cleaner. He had ropes, tranquilizers, tools, the works, right? You were right about his ID too. It was a fake and a good one. My people down south side haven't seen one that good in a while. It's not him of course, but then this is where it gets weird. The alias was off of a dead military contractor, a guy who got blown away in Afghanistan years ago. Your stiff's fingerprints were scorched off too, probably also done years ago."

"A real professional, huh?" Mr. Mercurio asked.

"Yeah, but not really the kind that would work with your old crew," Uncle Rolf replied. "I think you know this already."

"But it has to be!" Mr. Mercurio insisted. "I mean who else-"

"Look, Pop. They're all gone, man," Uncle Rolf interrupted. "The Capo, Alphonse, all the soldiers, I mean, it's all ancient history now. Even if any of them were still alive or not in jail, all their networks have been busted up for years. They think you're dead and they don't even know your boy exists. They never knew who turned them over. Look, we've been monitoring all correspondence and visits on the handful of people left in custody who had anything to do with you for decades now and they've given us nothing. Nothing! The ones still around probably don't even remember your name."

"But then who?... Why?..." Mr. Mercurio fumbled for words.

"Pop, think it over," Uncle Rolf continued. "The Buffalo crew's gone, buddy. I'm just a year and a half from retirement. I don't know who your stiff is, or how you're involved in his murder, and I don't think I want to know. But what I do know is that this guy's got nothing to do with you, OK?"

Mr. Mercurio slumped back in his chair, sighed, and furrowed his brow. Uncle Rolf stood up again, walked into the kitchen, and opened up his refrigerator.

"Here, Pop," he said and pulled out a couple cans of cheap beer. He opened both of them and handed one to Mr. Mercurio. Uncle Rolf toasted the cans together gently, sat down again, and they both took long sips. "There you go. Just calm down. Now let's think about this. Could your boy be mixed up with this guy?"

"No!" Mr. Mercurio blurted out instantly. Uncle Rolf looked at him incredulously until Mr. Mercurio quickly regained his composure and tried to reassure him. "You know little Vinnie. What kind of trouble could he possibly be mixed up in?"

Chapter Twelve

"The police are still not commenting on the identity of the victim except that he's a white male in his late fifties. This is Kate Lippold, live Eyewitness News. Back to you." she said with a bright, toothy smile into the camera.

"And... We're out," Tony chirped and lowered his camera off his shoulder. Kate's smile remained as they both started to walk back to their news van. Tony listened to the director in the studio through his earpiece. "Uh-huh... Uh-huh. Yeah, you got it nice and clean. OK... OK, I'll tell her. Did I give her too much headroom?... Fine. We're on our way."

"Boring!" she droned dreamily as she opened the van's side door.

"Fulmer says wipe that grin off your face, unless you want to go back to doing mornings," Tony said while he handed his camera to the technician inside the van.

"What?" she asked completely distracted.

"OK, that's it. I'm driving," he said as he climbed into the driver's seat. "Keep this up and you'll be drug tested."

"Must be the new boyfriend," the technician joked under his breath. Kate snapped out of it a little as they started to drive away.

"Hey!" she blurted.

"Oh yeah, everybody's heard about your swinger friend," Tony chuckled. "C'mon, Kate. We work for the news after all."

"Mmm. Vince," she grinned and took her cell phone out of her pocket. "I should call him right now. Think it's too soon?"

"Kate," Tony sighed. "You'll never make it to the anchor desk if you stay out all night partying with this guy all the time."

"Yeah, right. Watch me," Kate said coolly back to him. She dialed up Vince's number and listened into her phone for him to answer.

"She's trying his number. Stay close to them," Mr. Lockrom said and concentrated silently with his eyes fixed on his new laptops and a handful of crudely wired components, powered by a few car batteries. Mr. Rader's gaze remained centered on the back of the news van while they cruised down the street in their van, newly rented from U-Haul. "He's not answering. I've got nothing."

"Can't you triangulate his location at all? I thought you could do it even if his phone's off," Mr. Rader said and slowly pulled back a bit from tailing the news van, but kept them in sight.

"No. Not with this gear. Not if it wasn't on. Even with my old gear, we'd have to be within a few miles to find him when it was off and we know that those guys are hell and gone from here by now." Mr. Lockrom said back and took off his headset.

"Well, what have we got?" Mr. Rader asked.

"Just phone and internet," he replied, attempted to focus, and typed feverishly on one of his keyboards. "I've got traces on the girls, but nobody else yet. I'll have financial transactions and probably documentation by tomorrow."

"Probably?" Mr. Rader asked. As he grew angrier, his grip on the steering wheel grew tighter. "The clock's ticking here! We have to expand our search. They'll slip up somewhere."

Ferris, adorned in a thick, white bathrobe, guided Dave through the aftermath of his party. Dave looked hurried, but cheerful while Ferris yawned and rubbed his eyes. Ferris pointed at Jerry, passed out on one of his couches in the embrace of two naked ladies.

"Dude. Dude!" Dave raised his voice and lightly slapped him around. "Jerry! C'mon. Wake up! I've been looking forever for you idiots."

"Huh? Wha?" Jerry muttered as his eyes slowly came into focus and saw Dave above him. He sprung awake. "Ah! Dave!" His surprise was compounded when he noticed the two snoring, naked ladies on the couch on both sides of him, both too wasted to be roused by the commotion. "You... Uhh... You found us. I mean... We've been here all along. I mean, you didn't tell anybody we're here. Did you?"

"No," he replied and surveyed around the remains of Ferris' party. He stepped over a couple passed out ladies while he scanned the room and down the halls. "Where's Vince? I hope he's not in as bad shape as you are."

"Umm... Vince?" Jerry tried to stand up, but the weight of his hangover overpowered his shock. He sunk back down on the couch and clutched his forehead. "He's...Uhh... He's..."

"Dave!" Vince shouted as he jogged down a distant hall. "I knew I heard your voice. I thought I was dreaming. How are ya?"

"Worried!" he replied, left Jerry behind, and walked up to greet him. They hugged and Dave looked him up and down. "You OK? Don't come to Ferris' again without me. Take it from me. After midnight, this place will do you nothing but harm."

"Oh, I'm fit as a fiddle, D," Vince laughed and pointed at Jerry. "Besides, I can't compete with Casanova here. Good God! It looks like a civil war battlefield."

"Glad I got here when I did," Dave smiled and went on, "Got to get you boys cleaned up. I pulled some strings and landed you a primo spot tomorrow on the last night of the RAMP festival. Surprise show! We're talking at least twenty thousand people."

"Really?" Vince replied and arched an eyebrow. "That big shindig out in the Mojave?"

"For real, but we've gotta move quickly," Dave said. "The band's already on the road and we've got accommodations just outside of town. If we book, we can get settled in right before dinner. You down?"

"Whoa, whoa, whoa, whoa," Jerry stammered quickly and rose to his feet again. He took Vince aside and whispered in his ear, "I thought we were laying low until your father called. Remember the *paparazzi?*"

"C'mon, Vince!" Dave interjected stepping closer towards them and grew annoyed with Jerry's interference. "The timing is perfect! The buzz is out. People would kill for a shot like this. Trust me. I've seen this before. You sit on your hands now and it will take a lot longer to get big."

Before Vince could respond, Jerry said to both of them, "Look. Those vultures were all over us. We can't… Uhh… Just try to hide in some… Motel 6 in the middle of the desert."

"Wait!" Ferris butted in. "This is great! I've been waiting for a good excuse to take out my dad's new tricked out RV, man! We'll load the thing up all phat and take the party there, dawg."

"But-" Jerry tried to interrupt, but Dave beat him to it.

"Yeah, you'll be totally under the radar," Dave said with a widening grin. "Once you're inside, we'll get you in the VIP camp site. That place has more security than Fort Knox."

"You… You… Didn't tell anybody that we were here, did you?" Jerry asked.

"No! Damn, you're paranoid," Dave shot back.

"Hey. He's just looking out for me," Vince said and put his hands on Jerry's shoulders. "This is good, Jer. Hiding in plain sight. This way we can get these… *paparazzi* out in the open where they'll mind their manners."

"I don't know, Vince," Jerry hemmed and hawed. "It just feels like a bad idea."

"Why?" Dave asked bluntly. "You appear to be the only one here who thinks so. Why?"

"Umm…" Jerry froze up and eventually caved in, "I guess it's… It's safe to do this."

"Great!" Dave broke the anticipation with a clap of his hands.

"Sweet!" Ferris nearly jumped an inch off the ground in joy, "I gotta find Ali. Pack up the turntables for the ride."

"The ride?" Vince laughed. "I want you on stage with me."

"What?!" Ferris' eyes lit up.

"Man, those beats you threw down last night with my singing? We'll do, like, the last ten minutes of the set together," Vince moved over from Jerry and put his hands on Ferris' shoulders. "That was beautiful last night. We've practically invented a whole new genre. C'mon, let's get cleaned up. We'll practice on the way."

Ferris hugged Vince tightly, hysterical with laughter, and kissed him on the cheek.

"OK, OK, OK, big guy," Vince chuckled and patted him on the back. "Let's get rolling."

Vince and Ferris walked down a hall and laughed together. Dave picked up his cell phone and started to dial. Before Jerry could say something, Dave put the phone to his ear and went outside to get better reception. Stunned, Jerry just stood there, examined the ladies on the couch, and groaned as the weight of his hangover bore down on him again.

"Wait!" Mr. Lockrom said. "Mr. Liebowitz phone just came online and I think there's a call going out."

"Patch it in," Mr. Rader said and his eyes narrowed. "Let's hear it."

Chapter Thirteen

Ferris joined in on his turntables as they finished with a blissful version of "Summer Wind". For the first time in its history, the RAMP festival allowed Vince and his band a second encore. The roar of the crowd wouldn't stop, even after the soundmen started to pull the mics from their stands and the lights came up. Vince was exhausted but elated as he strutted off the stage with the band. They all hugged and congratulated each other, while their bodies cooled in the twilight desert air. They were met with a gauntlet of well-wishers, but Dave was in the front. He waited with a huge grin on his face and helped him through the crowd until they were clear.

"You did it! You did it!" Dave said gleefully.

"*We* did it! These boys!" Vince patted Ferris and each of the band members on the back. "You, me, Jerry, that crowd, man. It's a miracle! What a night. Well I'm totally spent. You boys sticking around?"

"Hell, yeah!" Troy said. "I'm gonna be knee deep in honeys by sunrise."

"Yeah, me too," Kevin agreed.

"You musicians. I don't know how you boys keep pace like this," Vince huffed and tried to catch his breath. "C'mon, Jerry. Let's go cool off back in the RV."

"Whoa-whoa-whoa. One more thing, boys." Dave stopped them before they could walk away. "There's a couple fellas from Rolling Stone want to get a few words and pictures in before the end of the night."

"Aww, man. Does it have to be tonight?" Vince whined.

"Twenty minutes, tops," Dave insisted. "This is big time! Trust me.

It's worth it. Ali's waiting with them back at the RV. Then you and Buzzkill here can go back to being boring, agreed?"

"Twenty minutes?" Jerry asked, insulted as usual by Dave.

"Scout's honor," Dave replied.

"Hey, I'll come too!" Ferris chimed in. "Maybe they'll put me on the cover with y'all."

"Fine. But I have a mind to not wait till tomorrow and split altogether," Vince said and walked away with Jerry and Ferris. "If I don't get some face time with Kate, I'm gonna flip out."

"Don't even think about it!" Dave shouted to Vince as he vanished through the crowds. "We got another photo shoot tomorrow! Get some rest!"

"C'mon, boss," Ayman smiled, put his arm around Dave, and led him in the opposite direction with Troy and Kevin to the after party tent.

Still elated from the show, Jerry, Vince, and Ferris giggled to each other, while they saluted and waved to the well-wishers who passed them. In the distance, they saw their massive RV just where they'd left it. Its front door open, a tall, dark figure up the steps was there to greet them. It was Mr. Rader, but instead of his black suit, he wore a Hawaiian shirt, beachcomber shorts, sandals, and a press laminate around his neck.

"Hi there! Great set guys!" he said warmly.

"You must be the Rolling Stone guy, eh?" Vince said and smiled. He entered first, shook Mr. Rader's hand, and passed by him as he walked into the back of the RV. Ferris followed him, as did Jerry, but Jerry paused after he passed Mr. Rader. There was a glint of recognition.

"Wait," Jerry mumbled to himself. "Where's his camera?"

They saw Ali, face down on one of the RV's couches and appeared to be asleep. Ferris shook him gently and laughed.

"You never could handle your liquor, could you, big guy?" Ferris joked, but suddenly felt a sharp pain on the side of his neck. He plucked out a small tranquilizer dart and had just enough time to stand up straight before he became woozy. Mr. Lockrom emerged from the shadows in the back of the RV as Ferris gradually passed out on the floor.

Startled, Jerry and Vince spun around, but before they could attempt an escape, Mr. Rader skillfully shot a single dart in each of their necks. By the time they slumped onto the floor too, Mr. Rader had already made his way to the driver's seat, started the RV's ignition and headlights, and started to pull away from the parking lot.

Back at the after party tent, the revelries were going full swing. Dave watched with perfect self-satisfaction as Ayman, Troy, and Kevin, danced suggestively, surrounded by a dozen scantily clad young ladies. He sipped on a glass of orange juice, but was interrupted with a tap on the shoulder. He glanced behind him to see Kate's smiling face.

"Hey girl!" he said and gave her a quick hug.

"Hi!" she shouted over the dance music and glanced around the tent. "Where's Vince? He's been good, hasn't he?"

"Oh, he's been an angel, despite all the temptations around here," Dave replied. "He's back at the RV giving an interview."

"I heard he'd be here, so I pulled some strings and got a press pass. I wanted to surprise him!" she said.

"Oh, he'll be overjoyed. Do you know where the RV is?" Dave asked.

"No. There's like a zillion of them out there." Kate answered.

"C'mon. I'll take you to him," Dave said and led her away from the tent. "You know, he was just telling me how much he was missing you."

"Aww, how sweet," she said in a playful, baby like tone.

They strolled passed several rows of trucks, cars, RVs, and such before turning a corner to find the empty space where Ferris' RV had been parked. Dave stopped in his tracks and looked around. He stamped his foot on the dusty ground, immediately took out his cell phone, and started to dial.

"I knew it. I knew it," He grumbled angrily under his voice. "I bet Jerry talked him into this, that god damn idiot."

"What's wrong?" Kate asked. "Where are they?"

"Hey! … Stupid voice mail," Dave blurted into his phone before he could answer her. He paused and waited for the beep. "Vince! You morons! I told you to wait until tomorrow! That photo shoot's coming out of your next royalty check if you're not back here by 8 AM sharp! Oh, and Kate's here too if you need a better reason, you prima donna! Vince, I love you, but will you trust me just once?! I'm going to call back every hour on the hour until I hear from you!"

Dave hung up his phone, put it back in his pocket, and pulled out a prescription bottle. He struggled with the cap until Kate gently took it from him, calmly removed the cap, and handed the bottle back to him.

"Thanks, sorry about that," Dave said before he swallowed a couple pills. He shook his head, shrugged his shoulders, took a deep breath, and pointed back to the direction of the tent. "The least I could do is get you a drink. Coming?"

"Yeah, I guess," she said, clearly disappointed, and followed him.

"Looks like he's starting to come around." Mr. Lockrom glanced over to Ali while he quickly typed on one of his laptops. "I thought you said the dose was good for at least an hour."

Mr. Rader caught sight in his center rear view mirror of Ali, who began to groan and squirm. Ali was blindfolded, gagged, and bound at the wrists and ankles with thick zip ties, just like Ferris, Vince, and Jerry in the back of the RV. Mr. Rader's blank expression didn't change and he refocused his eyes on the road ahead of him.

"Never mind that. Just find something on him," Mr. Rader said back.

"Are you sure this is government issue?" Mr. Lockrom asked. He stopped typing on his laptop for a moment and held up a small, black semi-automatic pistol.

"I know one when I see one. Keep looking," he replied.

Ali was awake enough to hear the last sentence and felt that his left pant leg had been pulled halfway up his calf and his pistol was missing from his ankle holster. As the reality of the situation slowly sank in, Ali hung his head down in despair.

"I think I got something. Wait just a second!" Mr. Lockrom's eyes lit up under his thick glasses and the pace of his typing quickened. The commotion was just enough to start to wake Ferris, Vince, and Jerry.

"It's about time," Mr. Rader grumbled.

"That's gratitude for you," Mr. Lockrom gave him a bitter sneer. "I crack the FBI database with these rinky-dink tinker toys and you make it sound like I'm goofing off on Farmville."

"Feds?" Mr. Rader's interest perked up. "You sure?"

"Well, he's on their payroll anyway," Mr. Lockrom replied. "Probably an informant. He looks a little young for an agent."

"That's just great. How in the hell did they catch on to this before us?" Mr. Rader mumbled to himself. "OK, whatever. We'll interrogate after the drop off. What about Mr. Spencer's recorder? Anything?"

The others were awake enough to hear now and Jerry too grunted in protest upon hearing what Mr. Rader said.

"That sounds promising," Mr. Rader said.

"Just finishing the upload now. Two seconds," Mr. Lockrom said and switched to another laptop that was connected to Jerry's recorder through a USB cable. "Alright. Let's have a listen. This might save us all a lot of time. Here's the last entry."

Mr. Lockrom turned up the volume on his laptop enough so

everyone in the RV could hear. Jerry started to panic as he heard his recorded voice. "Wednesday, well Thursday now. 2:14 AM. I still have no idea whatsoever how the V3 formula brought Vince back from the dead."

Ferris and Ali stopped struggling so they could listen and Vince was wide awake and tried to sit up. Jerry lightly banged his head on the floor of the RV in frustration as the voice continued, "Even if I knew, that is just the beginning. His new found singing talent, his steady improvement in physical fitness, that... that *ANNOYING* new upbeat attitude!"

Mr. Lockrom stopped the recording when he heard Vince's muffled shouting from underneath his gag. He looked to Mr. Rader, who glanced at him through the rear view mirror and eventually nodded. Mr. Lockrom pulled Vince's gag down to his neck.

"What the hell's going on here?!" Vince shouted. His head whipped around in an effort to get a bearing on where everyone was. "Jerry! Jerry! What the hell?! You gave me the formula?! How could you do this to me?! Why didn't you tell me?! What have you gotten us into?!"

Jerry struggled to speak through his gag as well. Mr. Lockrom laughed out loud.

"Oh, man. I've got to hear this. May I?" He asked Mr. Rader. After a couple seconds, he responded.

"Fine," Mr. Rader said. The instant Jerry's gag was removed, he spoke.

"Vince! Vince! I'm sorry! I'm so sorry, man!" Jerry shouted. The racket was already starting to annoy Mr. Rader. "I had no choice! I wasn't thinking! I couldn't revive you and I panicked!"

"Why didn't you tell me!?!" Vince shouted.

"I...I... ", Jerry stammered. "You didn't remember anything! I was the only one who knew about the formula! I didn't want this getting out!"

"You wanted this for yourself!" Vince accused him. "I know you!

You thought this could make you rich! Didn't you?!"

"Make *US* rich! I was totally going to share it with you!" Jerry shot back.

"Oh, yeah?!" Vince shouted. "And just when were you going to let me in on this, huh?!"

"When I could make it work again!" Jerry shouted back and grew angry. "You heard what I said on the recording! I don't know how it did what it did! I still don't!"

"What it *DID*?!" Vince shouted. "I'm dead, Jerry! I'm a dead man! *DEAD*! I'm not even me anymore! I… I… I trusted you, god damn it!"

"That's it!" Mr. Rader finally butted in. "They're giving me a headache. Gag em'."

"Screw you!" Jerry shouted and struggled as Mr. Lockrom tried to put his gag back in,

"Yeah?! Well, screw you, too!" Vince yelled back.

"Not you! Them!" Jerry got in just before Mr. Lockrom managed to cover his mouth again with the gag.

"Screw you *AND* them, you stupid bastards!" Vince screamed at the top of his lungs. "Let go of me!!!"

But it was no use and Mr. Lockrom put Vince's gag back on his mouth again. Jerry and Vince, both having an approximate idea of where each other were in the RV by then, continued to shout underneath their gags at each other.

Ali leaned forward, jerked his head back, while he made a noise that clearly was a muffled "Hey", in an attempt to get Mr. Rader's attention. This went on for a few seconds, before Mr. Rader looked back at Mr. Lockrom again through the rear view mirror and reluctantly nodded.

"OK, but you better tell me something I want to hear," Mr. Rader said. "And if you shout half as loud as they did, I'll will personally kick your ass."

Mr. Lockrom smirked, rolled his eyes, and took down Ali's gag. Ali took a deep breath and tried to remain calm.

"OK… OK…" Ali said. "Thank you. Look… It's clear that none of us know who you are, what you look like, why you want us, anything. If you let us go, there's a very good chance that you both will get away scott free. If you don't, my people will hunt you down, you hear me?"

"Gag," Mr. Rader blurted simply.

Before Ali could get out another word, Mr. Lockrom put his gag back in and for fun, he gave Ali a swift slap on the back of his head. Ali protested underneath his gag, but it only made Mr. Lockrom laugh.

"Look, guys," Mr. Rader addressed his captives. "Let's get something straight here. We're just the mules. Very soon, I will no longer care who you are, what you know, or what your people…" He put up one hand and made a quotation mark sign. "Will do to me. After tonight, you're no longer my problem."

Chapter Fourteen

Vince, Jerry, Ferris, and Ali could hear and feel the RV slow down as it pulled off the freeway. After a couple stops and turns, they could tell they were on a quiet, winding road, and could feel the RV slow down more on the hairpin turns.

"Finally," Mr. Rader said wearily to himself as the RV finally came to a complete stop. He turned back to Mr. Lockrom. "You wanna get the gate?"

"Looks like they know we're here already," he replied. "Lots more security guys tonight than usual."

"Oh, goodie," Mr. Rader said under his breath and the others could hear the faint buzz of an electric gate's motor. The RV pulled through and they drove slowly for about a half-minute before they stopped for good. Mr. Rader shut off the engine and joined the rest in the back. "We can cut their feet loose now. They've got nowhere to run."

They took out pocketknives and Mr. Rader cut the thick zip ties at the feet of Vince and Jerry, while Mr. Lockrom cut those of Ferris and Ali. They stood them all on their feet, grabbed the backs of their collars, and led them out of the RV's side door.

"C'mon. You're almost there," Mr. Lockrom said and after a few steps, halted them. "Gentlemen, we have arrived."

They heard several footsteps approach them and each captive felt a hand placed on one of their elbows. They were pulled forcibly at first, and then gentler as each of them co-operated. They could tell that they were led indoors after they heard a large door shut behind them. Their footsteps echoed on the marble floors of a cool, cavernous, winding corridor. At one turn, Mr. Lockrom separated from the group and took Ferris and Ali in another direction.

"Second door on the left, correct?" he asked.

"Correct. Meet me in the lab when they're secure," Mr. Rader replied.

Mr. Lockrom led them into a room, cut the zip ties around their hands, and they were released.

"You can take off your gags and blindfolds now," he said to Ferris and Ali. They did what he said and after a couple seconds, their eyes adjusted to the light and focused. They could see they were in a large waiting room with fancy, modern furniture, and marble walls with no windows. "Have a seat. I'd tell you not to go anywhere, but I think you've figured that out already. We'll be with you again shortly."

Mr. Lockrom left them in the room, shut and locked the door behind him. Ferris and Ali inspected the room briefly before they spoke.

"What the hell's going on here?!" Ferris whispered forcefully. "Why'd he say you're a snitch?"

"I'm not a snitch!" he shot back, also in a forced whisper.

"Well, Why are you spying on me then?" Ferris accused him. "Why are these guys after Vince and Jerry?"

"I don't know and I'm not spying on you… I'm spying on your dad," Ali said. He finally gave up looking for another way out and sat down on one of the room's leather chairs.

"But you've never even met my dad. He's never home," Ferris said and calmed down a little.

"Yeah, I know. But the Bureau sent me in anyway to see if I can find out anything about his finances," Ali said.

"His finances? What, are you screwing with me?" Ferris asked incredulously.

"No, for real," Ali insisted. "We were looking to see if he had any illegal business going on in Iran. You know your family has some friends on the Islamic Council."

"The hell I did!" Ferris blurted out. "What do I care? My dad hardly says two words to me whenever he's around, which is hardly ever. Do you think he tells me anything? I just spend his money. He'd kick my ass if I ever asked where he got it. Oh man, what do you think they'll do to us?"

"I don't know," Ali said and his voice grew grave. "I just hope it's quick."

Down the hall from them, Vince and Jerry were led into another room. Vince's hands were still bound, but Mr. Rader removed his blindfold and gag. His pistol pointed at Vince's head, he placed his other hand on Vince's shoulder and forced him to sit on an ordinary plastic chair. Vince didn't say anything as he watched a couple men in black suits lead Jerry onto a surgical table, where they freed him from the zip ties on his hands, but strapped his ankles and wrists down with thick, leather restraints before they removed his blindfold and gag. Both of them could tell they were in a huge tiled room, filled with state of the art medical equipment, but couldn't make out much else, since they'd pointed bright surgical lamps at both of them. Jerry was about to say something when the door opened again, this time automatically.

They watched a thin man in an electric wheelchair at the end of the long hall as he approached slowly, followed by a couple men dressed in full surgical gear. One of the men bumped into a vase on a pedestal in the hallway, which caused it to teeter slightly, but it quickly settled.

"Oh, do be careful with that, you klutz. That's a Ming vase, worth more than you've made in your entire life," the man in the wheelchair scolded him in a weak, raspy voice. He turned his attention to Vince and Jerry as they entered the room and the door closed behind them again. "Mr. Mercurio, Mr. Spencer. You two are very difficult men to get hold of and much more resourceful than expected."

"Sod it, Mansell!" a voice shouted from the other side of the room.

They all looked over and saw Mr. Cunningham hobble in on his crutches from a door on the opposite side of the room. "We got the bloody package here. Now where's our money?"

"Mansell?" Jerry asked, squinted at the man in the wheelchair, and struggled to make out his face. "Dr. Michael Mansell?"

"We've been kidnapped by our old boss?" Vince asked.

"Oh, kidnapped is such an ugly word, young man," Dr. Mansell said dryly. "After all, tonight, I will be granting you both the once in a lifetime chance to change the world forever. Look, we know you used the V3 formula on Mr. Mercurio, right? We know it works on a cellular level too. We know that you, Mr. Spencer, have been working to replicate what happened ever since, as we have. And as you can see, our equipment is far more sophisticated, and our people much smarter than you."

"Then what do you need us for?" Jerry asked.

"I need to know how you did it," Dr. Mansell demanded and he moved his wheelchair closer to him. The surgical lights revealed his long, sickly face.

"I don't know! I didn't know it would work then. I still don't know if it was the formula that brought him back to life in the first place!" Jerry pleaded and squirmed weakly under his restraints.

"Oh, he just came back to life on his own then?" Dr. Mansell asked sarcastically.

"Well, yes. Maybe," Jerry stammered and attempted to find the right words. "It's... It's not impossible that a person who flat-lined as long as he did could eventually come round again. I... Uhh... Can't think of... Uhh... Well, I remember hearing about that one kid who fell through that hole in the ice in Minnesota that-"

"Rubbish!" Dr. Mansell interrupted him. "Not at room temperature, not for that long."

"Look," Vince finally spoke up. "Just let my friends go. You can do whatever you want to me. I shouldn't be alive anyway. Take any samples you want, any tests done. Hell, just go ahead and dissect me."

"That's very tempting, Mr. Mercurio, but I'm afraid there's not enough time for that," Dr. Mansell said. He was distracted for a second by Mr. Lockrom, who sat in the corner. His fingers tapped on his laptop keyboard loudly and the sound echoed in the room while he typed. "Must you insist on doing that now?"

"Sorry," Mr. Lockrom replied. "Just catching up on some e-mails. I'll try to type quieter."

"Dad? What are you doing?" Lonnie asked calmly as she entered the room, instantly attracting the attention of everybody except Mr. Lockrom.

"Lonnie!" Jerry smiled wide and tried to raise his head. "Thank God you're here. Your dad, he… He…" Jerry's voice trailed off as he noticed Lonnie's blank expression.

"Oh, boy," Vince said and he hung his head down.

"You said you wouldn't hurt them," she said accusingly.

"I haven't and I won't, pumpkin. I promise," Dr, Mansell consoled her. "As long as they tell me what I need to know. You see, boys, as you probably noticed by my rather decrepit appearance, that I am dying. As we speak, terminal cancers in multiple organs are closing in on me. So I did what any ordinary billionaire scientist would do and had his entire company down to the man working on this project in an effort to reverse my condition."

"But we weren't told why we were working on this," Vince said.

"Of course you weren't. Why should you've been told?" Dr. Mansell answered immediately. "You were the lowest on the totem pole, but yet you figured this out all by yourselves."

"I'm telling you, we didn't! It was an accident!" Jerry insisted.

"I don't believe you, but I shall soon know the truth," Dr. Mansell said bluntly. He looked at one of the men in surgical gear and pointed at Jerry's feet. The man took off Jerry's shoes and socks, though Jerry tried to resist, the restraints made it impossible.

"Dad, you promised," Lonnie demanded and stepped closer. "I

mean... He's not like the others. Jerry's really sweet. Can't we let him go?"

Jerry's eyes met Lonnie's for a moment and they smiled at each other.

"Not yet, dear. He'll be fine. This will only take a moment," Dr, Mansell said, turned his chair slightly, and grabbed a small, white, unlabeled aerosol can on a tray of surgical instruments. "Actually, I wanted to show you this anyway, one of my new toys. I'm considering selling it to the military. Faster than water boarding and without the mess, unless of coarse he messes himself. Damn. I forgot to bring the diapers."

"What are you going to do to me?!" Jerry asked in desperation.

"Stay still please. Just one moment," Dr. Mansell said and sprayed a thin, transparent mist onto the bottoms of both of Jerry's bare feet. "There. That wasn't so bad now, was it?"

"Oh, I... Uhh... " Jerry, nearly at the point of hyperventilation from panic, tried to control his breath. "No, I... what did you do to me? It doesn't hurt... I mean... There's a slight tingling... It's just..."

He looked up to see that Dr. Mansell was holding a long eagle's feather in his hand. He smiled devilishly as he brushed the feather gently over Jerry's left foot. Jerry erupted in hysterical laughter, so loud it took everybody in the room except Dr. Mansell by surprise.

"Ah! I love it. Works every time," Dr. Mansell said proudly. "I'm still working on a more clever name for it, but I like to call it 'Laffatitall'."

Vince groaned and sunk his head again.

"Yes, I admit, puns are corny," Dr. Mansell went on. "You see, Mr. Spencer. You will tell me what you know eventually, so you best just spit it out now."

"I don't know anything!" Jerry insisted, while he concentrated desperately to control his laughter and catch his breath. Dr, Mansell tickled him again and Jerry burst instantly into hysterical laughter, even louder than before.

"Stop it!" Vince pleaded, but was ignored by everybody.

"Now you had to have done something, anything," Dr. Mansell pressed on. "We've tried different shock voltages, different doses, time intervals, temperatures. You did something different that night. What was it?"

"I don't know!" Jerry screamed, gasped for air, with a painful and contorted grin plastered across his face. "Oh God! Please stop! I swear I don't know!"

Dr. Mansell rolled his eyes and tickled Jerry again. He kept going until Lonnie finally grabbed her father's hand and pulled it away.

"Pumpkin!" he scolded her.

"Please, Daddy!" she pouted. "I really like this one."

Jerry's abdomen flexed in intense pain as he looked up at Lonnie and nodded furiously. He was barely able to breathe.

"You monster!" Vince yelled. "This is America! You can't torture people!"

"You don't keep up with current events much, do you?" Dr. Mansell quipped and was just about to tickle Jerry again.

"If this is going to take long, I could use a cup of coffee," Mr. Rader complained.

"*WAIT*! *WAIT*! *THAT'S IT*!" Jerry screamed at the top of his voice. Dr. Mansell backed away for a moment. "Coffee! Vince and I had coffee just before it happened!"

"Coffee, eh?" Dr. Mansell thought to himself for a few seconds. "Hmm. Well, yes, well… That actually does explain a few things."

"The formula must have needed to bind with the caffeine or something to be effective enough to work on a whole organism!" Jerry said as he gasped desperately for air. "It had to be the catalyst."

"Hmm." Dr. Mansell thought further. He motioned forward for a second and considered tickling Jerry again. Jerry recoiled, but Dr. Mansell leaned back in his wheelchair and thought to himself again. He motioned forward one more time for a second, but backed down again, and finally put away the feather. Vince, Lonnie, and especially Jerry let out a huge sigh of relief.

"Brilliant theory!" Dr. Mansell clapped and rubbed his hands together. "I should have thought of that myself." He turned to his daughter and took her hand in one, gently patted it with the other. "I do like this one too, darling. Would you be a dear and brew up a pot of coffee. I wouldn't ask, but I gave the house staff the night off for this special occasion."

"Well, OK," she replied reluctantly while she walked out of the room. "I hope I remember how to work the machine."

"And make sure to use the good beans!" he shouted towards her direction after a few seconds. "You know, the Jamaican stuff! Thanks!" Dr. Mansell then leaned over to one of the men in surgical gear and spoke softly. "Prep one of the mice. I want to see this work first."

"Sir... I... " Jerry spoke up. "I mean, even if it works on the mouse. It doesn't mean that it's going to work on you."

"I'm willing to take that chance and as you can see, I can't wait any longer, " he answered immediately. "Unless you'd rather have us test it on you?" Dr, Mansell looked at one of the men in surgical gear with bright eyes.

"Oh, no!" Jerry said right away. "It's just... I mean, I'm sure it'll work. It's just that we can't predict what it will do to you. Vince here was young and in perfect health."

"So you think it'll make me worse then?" Dr. Mansell chuckled. "No, my dear boy. I've got days to go, not weeks. I'm high as a kite on painkillers and even they are not working anymore."

"But haven't you lived a full life already?" Jerry asked.

"I'm only fifty-two," Dr. Mansell answered.

"Oh... Well... I... " Jerry found himself at a loss of words.

"Mr. Rader. If you would be so kind as to escort these gentlemen to the other room to join their friends," Dr. Mansell said and nodded to the men in surgical gear, who began to release Jerry from his restraints. He tapped Jerry on the shoulder before he rolled away towards one of the surgical workstations. "Oh, and do be careful when putting your shoes and socks back on your feet. The drug will wear off in a few minutes."

"If this works, will you let us go free?" Vince asked.

"Certainly. Why shouldn't I?" Dr. Mansell replied, his back turned to him. "Nobody would believe your story anyway if you told them. Besides, if these gentlemen wouldn't hunt you down, my lawyers most assuredly would."

"Oh," Vince said, thought for a moment, and asked, "Well, what happens to us if it doesn't work?"

"Hmmm." Dr. Mansell stopped his wheelchair gradually, turned his head slightly in his direction, and pointed to Mr. Rader. "I guess I'll just leave it up to him then, shall I?"

"You can't do that!" Jerry pleaded. "You'd never get away with it!"

"Oh, sure I would. I have an incinerator in the basement," Dr. Mansell replied coolly and turned away from them.

Vince made a slight gulping sound and looked up to Mr. Rader nervously from his seat. Mr. Rader glanced down at him for a moment, but his expression remained blank. Jerry was now free from his restraints and began to slowly put on his socks. He clenched his teeth and tried not to laugh out loud.

"You… Uhh…" Vince struggled to speak to Mr. Rader. "Did you like my music?"

After a pause that felt like forever to Vince and Jerry, Mr. Rader shrugged one shoulder, nodded, and replied casually, "Yeah, you were pretty good actually."

Chapter Fifteen

In the waiting room, Ali and Ferris continued their conversation. They exhausted any ideas of escape, so they attempted half heartedly to relax and lounged on a couple of the room's many leather chairs.

"So why the Bureau?" asked Ferris.

"Well, I tried the army after 9/11, but they turned me down," Ali replied. "It wasn't enough that I was young, in shape, and fluent in Arabic, Farsi, and Pashtun. I just wanted to do my part like everybody else."

"So why'd they turn you down?" Ferris pressed on.

"Well… uhh…" Ali drifted off a moment. "I guess at the time I shouldn't have asked if it'd be a problem that I was dating a guy."

"You like guys?" Ferris looked surprised.

"Well, I like girls too," Ali said quickly. "I mean, C'mon. You've seen me with the ladies. You've must have caught me in the act twice at least."

"Way more," Ferris added, but hesitated as he went on. "But… I mean, all that time. Were you thinking?… Well, did you want me?"

"No. Not really," Ali said, noticed Ferris' confused expression, and quickly added. "You're not a bad looking guy and you can take that just as a compliment. It's just you're just not my type."

"Oh. Thanks, … I guess," Ferris said. Having felt reassured, he spoke again. " So you didn't find anything on my dad, huh?"

"Zilch," he replied and made a zero shape with his thumb and index finger. "I'd actually been leading the Bureau along for a while just so I could keep hanging out with you."

"Really?" Ferris asked.

"Yeah, I mean, c'mon, ever since I met you, I've been having the time of my life." Ali smiled and patted his shoulder. "Really, I wish this assignment could go on forever!"

"Well, quit the Bureau!" Ferris laughed. "I'll double what they're paying you and make you my personal bodyguard."

They both heard footsteps approach from outside and they quickly stood up.

"If we live through this, I might just take you up on that," Ali said grimly. "My track record of protecting you hasn't been that good so far."

Ali and Ferris braced themselves as the door opened, but were relieved to see it was just Jerry and Vince. As they entered the room, Jerry let out little muffled snickering sounds after every step he took.

"What's so funny?" Ali asked after the door was closed again.

"Nothing. I promise you that. They've drugged me. I can't help it," Jerry said and sighed in relief as he sat down on a chair and raised his feet off the ground.

"We're in deep trouble, guys," Vince said.

"No kidding," Ferris said.

"We've got to think of something quick! We've got to stop them!" Jerry said in a forced whisper, and waved his hands downwards in an effort to quiet down the others.

"How? We're screwed," Ali disregarded him and spoke normally while he paced around the room. "What did you get us into Jerry?"

"Look, everybody. I'm sorry, OK? This is all my fault. At first, it was just to save Vince," Jerry spoke up and begged sincerely. He counted out numbers on his fingers as he went on. "But then, I didn't know it would go this far. I didn't consider the consequences. I had stars in my eyes. I thought this would make us rich and famous! Dear God! I'd give anything to be a research scientist again!"

"What? So you didn't like being my manager?" Vince asked sarcastically.

"Of all times, you're going to bring this up now?" Jerry asked resentfully, and then apologized. "Look, I'm sorry. I'm just not cut out for show business, OK?"

Before either could speak again, the lights dimmed suddenly and then came back on. Vince and Jerry gave each other a knowing look.

"Oh no," Vince said in disbelief.

"Already?" Jerry replied. "The mouse must have worked instantly. He's gone and done it."

"What?" Ferris and Ali both asked almost at the same time.

"Dr. Mansell, he's attempting to be born again, like Vince," Jerry said and looked at an antique clock across the room.

"Lonnie's dad is behind this?" Ferris asked but Vince ignored him and looked at the clock too.

"How long?" he asked Jerry quickly.

"I don't know. It took over twenty minutes with you, but it took a couple minutes before I could inject the formula. Also, you were in good health-"

"Good health? I was totally out of shape," Vince interrupted and patted his stomach with both hands.

"Yeah, but you weren't sick, not Dr. Mansell sick," Jerry quickly replied. "Even if it does work, we have no idea what it will do to him. It might do nothing. Then again, it could give rise to an incurable, contagious, super-flu or something. And what if it **DOES** bring him back and cure him? What then? What if it gives him special powers like Vince?"

"Special powers?" Vince asked resentfully.

"Well... Like your voice," Jerry responded.

"But I never really tried singing before. How do you know I didn't do that myself?" Vince asked.

"Huh," Jerry paused. "Yeah, good point. Sorry. Then again, maybe we're both right. Maybe you always had the talent and the formula just released it."

"Nice!" Ferris joked. "I want to try it. I bet I'd be a great porn star."

"Or a good florist," Vince said.

"What?" Ferris asked quickly.

"Well, you've never tried it," Vince said back.

Everybody but Jerry chuckled nervously for a moment. Jerry started to case the room for an exit.

"We've tried that already," Ali said. "Don't bother."

"Can't you do anything? Aren't you a Fed or something?" Jerry asked as he paced and his hands grew jittery.

"Well, Why don't you think of something, Mr. Genius Scientist," Ali retorted. "They've got my weapon. We have no phones. And even if we did, we have no idea where we are."

"But we do know," Vince said. "We must be at Dr. Mansell's estate. We couldn't have been driving for more than three hours. I know it's somewhere near the ocean around here. You all heard the waves walking in, right? Isn't it up near San Luis Obispo? San Simeon or somewhere?"

"No idea. Besides, even if somebody believed us, who'd get here in time to stop this?" Ali replied. After a long grim pause, Vince spoke.

"Well, if it works, he said he'd let us go," he said.

"Vince... ," Jerry stood in front of him and put his hands on Vince's shoulders. "The formula brought you back. I will always be grateful for that. But if it really works, and it becomes public now, it's going to unleash terrible consequences."

"Like what?" Ferris laughed. "This thing sounds awesome! You get to live forever and you have special powers. What's wrong? We won't be able to walk around during the daytime?"

"No! Well... I don't know... " Jerry stammered. "I mean, think about it. People will pay anything for it. Nations would fight over it. There'd be a race war between the Born-Agains versus the... Uhh... First ... Timers?"

There was another long pause and they all thought silently.

"First Timers. I guess that works," Vince said blandly.

"Wait… Wait…" Ferris stood transfixed in thought. "Give me a minute and I'll think of something cool… How about Virgins?"

"That's good," Vince perked up for a second. "Virgins. I like that. Let's go with that."

Before Jerry could speak again, they all paused after they heard footsteps approach again from outside in the hall. Jerry and Vince gave each other confused looks.

"It worked?" Vince asked.

"Impossible," Jerry replied quickly and started to back away from the room's door, as the footsteps grew louder. "Way too soon."

"They'd still be waiting if it didn't, right?" Ali asked.

"Maybe it killed him," Jerry said.

The door swung open and Mr. Cunningham hobbled in on his crutches, flanked by Mr. Rader who stood in the doorway, once again dressed in his black suit. Mr. Cunningham had a mean look in his eyes as he headed straight towards Jerry. Jerry's eyes bugged out the moment he realized that he had nowhere left to back away to and stopped when his back touched a wall. The others stood still as Mr. Cunningham halted his advance just a couple feet away from Jerry. He stared at Jerry cruelly with his icy, blue eyes and without warning, whipped his pistol out from his shoulder holster, cocked its hammer, and put the barrel just inches from Jerry's forehead. Jerry clenched his eyelids shut as hard as he could and shuttered in terror.

"*NO!*" Vince shouted.

Vince, Ferris, and Ali all flinched as Mr. Cunningham laughed mischievously, uncocked the pistol, and put it back in his shoulder holster.

"Ah, I got ya', you wanker!" Mr. Cunningham laughed even more as he backed away, taking a second to point at Vince, Ferris, and Ali with one of his crutches. "Dr. Mansell is alive and well. He wants to see you all."

"You bastard!" Jerry's eyes sprung open again and he backed up off from the wall.

"Thanks. I feel better already," Mr. Cunningham said to Mr. Rader, who snickered a little himself. He turned back to the others and beckoned them, by cocking his head towards the door. "C'mon now. That's for all the trouble you tossers put us all through."

Mr. Rader took the lead in front of the group, while Mr. Cunningham kept up on his crutches from the rear. Jerry tried to whisper to Vince.

"Something's has to be wrong, man," he said while he kept his head down.

"I can totally hear you," Mr. Rader said bluntly, not even looking back at them.

"Fine!" Jerry spoke up and cleared his throat. "He shouldn't have come back by now. We could all be in danger."

"We're already in danger, you moron!" Ali said. "Just do or say whatever they want and we might all walk out of here alive."

"But... But... " Jerry protested weakly, but piped down just as they re-entered Dr. Mansell's laboratory.

"Eureka! Success!" Dr. Mansell shouted from his wheelchair. They were caught off guard to hear that his voice was at least twice as loud as earlier, clear and well annunciated, and without a hint of wheezing. He rolled over towards Jerry. One of his masked assistants struggled to keep up behind him while he pushed along a rolling IV bag stand attached to Dr. Mansell's arm. He stretched out that arm and paid no notice of the IV to shake Jerry's hand. The strength of his grip shocked Jerry and caused him to wince slightly. "Thank you! Thank you! A thousand times, thank you!"

"Uhh..." Jerry was at a loss of words and looked to Vince, who desperately, but discreetly made a silent gesture to carry on. "You're welcome, sir."

"I feel better than I've felt in years," Dr. Mansell finally released

Jerry's hand and then smiled at his daughter who lingered in the back of the lab. "Oh honey, you finally brought home one I like."

Lonnie blushed as she giggled, winked at Jerry, gave him a little wave, and said, "Hi!" under her breath. Jerry waved back trancelike, still in shock from the situation. Mr. Lockrom, who still typed on his laptop in the same chair he was in earlier, looked up for a moment, chortled deridingly, and continued to type.

"Son, you and your friends are free to go," Dr. Mansell smiled wider and wider as he spoke. He motioned to one of his masked assistants and they handed out envelopes to Mr. Rader, Lockrom, and Cunningham. Mr. Lockrom didn't get up from his chair, pocketed the envelope in his jacket, and continued to type. "Well done, gentlemen, despite the setbacks. I think you'll find the bonus I added more than generous for your troubles. And Jerry, because I'm so impressed with you and I'm in **SUCH** a good mood, I want you back tomorrow at my lab bright and early!"

"Well... Uhh... Thank you, Dr. Mansell." Jerry agreed reluctantly.

"Oh, call me Mike!" Dr. Mansell laughed and grew more excited. He started to fidget in his wheelchair. "And no more busy work for you, lad. I'm sending you right to the top with me. You're going to get everything you've ever wanted from this little formula. We'll be rich! Well, you'll be rich and I'll be even richer! HA! HA! HA! HA!"

Jerry, Vince, Ferris, and Ali all feigned laughter and joined Dr. Mansell, who's breath became longer and heavier as the seconds passed. While he laughed, Dr. Mansell slapped his knee and saw it bounce up a couple of inches.

"Whoa!" Dr. Mansell stopped laughing and his eyes bugged out in awe. "Did you see that?! My legs! I can move them again!"

Lonnie stepped up quickly from the back of the room and took her father's side, amazed and watched closely.

"Do they hurt?" she asked.

"Why... No," her father replied cheerfully. "I know the muscles should have atrophied to jelly by now, but they feel great! Strong. In fact, hold on a second."

He motioned as if he was going to stand, but Lonnie put her hand on his shoulder and held him down. He gently took her hand off.

"Just trust me," he said confidently. Astounded, Jerry inched forward as they all watched Dr. Mansell steadily rise out of his wheelchair. Both he and Lonnie flinched forward for a second, as it looked as though Dr. Mansell was going to lose his balance for a moment. Dr. Mansell put his hands up instantly. "No! No. I can do this... Watch."

They backed off as he inhaled deeply, straightened his back, and pushed the wheelchair away from behind him.

"Abracadabra!" Dr. Mansell proudly announced and laughed.

Everybody in the room was speechless as they watched except for Mr. Lockrom, who finally stopped typing, closed his laptop, stood up, and started to walk towards the exit. He stopped when he noticed Dr. Mansell.

"Whoa. He's standing," Mr. Lockrom said casually.

"Can I get a High Five?!" Dr. Mansell asked and put his hand up, barely able to contain his excitement. Mr. Lockrom seemed annoyed by the request, but was about to slap his hand, when he heard his smart phone beep in his jacket.

"Ooops! Hold that thought. I've gotta check this text." Mr. Lockrom took his smart phone out of his pocket, turned his back to him, and started to walk toward the exit again.

"Why you little! ..." Dr. Mansell's excitement from joy, started gradually to switch to anger, and it grew stronger.

"Um, dude," Ferris finally spoke up. "I wouldn't leave him hanging, man."

"Everybody stay still!" Mr. Rader blurted out.

Mr. Lockrom ignored them, fiddled with his smart phone, and tucked his laptop under his other arm. As Dr. Mansell's breath grew deeper and louder, his entire body mass started to very gradually grow larger. Veins and muscles gently pulsated with every breath, and his skin color faded until it was almost pure white. Everybody else in the lab was stunned, and just when Lonnie attempted to speak, Dr. Mansell lunged forward, and snatched Mr. Lockrom's smart phone from his hand.

"Hey!" Mr. Lockrom protested. "What the hell?!"

Mr. Lockrom's anger instantly turned to fear as he turned around and witnessed Dr. Mansell continue to grow larger and heard his breath grow more forceful. He clenched the smart phone in his iron grip. Everybody else flinched and took a step back, as the phone finally shattered into a dozen pieces like a wine glass.

"*HA! HA! HA! HA!*" Dr. Mansell bellowed and threw the shards of the phone over his shoulder. They almost hit Mr. Rader in the face, but he ducked his head left just in time to avoid them.

"Dad! Stop!" Lonnie begged as she advanced forward a step, but then retreated when her father turned to face her. Everybody could hear a faint, eerie, creaking noise, as all of Dr. Mansell's bones began to grow longer, which made him grow gradually taller as his body mass grew.

"*I FEEL WONDERFUL! I FEEL-*" Dr. Mansell ranted and his voice grew louder, huskier, and deeper, until suddenly he started to shout gibberish. "*RAGGA FRAGGA RAGGA FA HA GA FRAGGA!!!*"

"Jesus Christ!" Mr. Lockrom shouted.

Dr. Mansell whipped around to face him again, snatched his laptop from under his arm, and clubbed Mr. Lockrom over the head with it. Everybody else recoiled in horror, except Mr. Rader who stayed still, as Mr. Lockrom keeled over, struck unconscious before he even hit the ground. Lonnie screamed as her father continued to bash Mr. Lockrom's head in with the laptop fourteen more times, until the pieces of his head and laptop mingled together, which littered the floor in a bloody mess.

"Oh, that's it," Mr. Cunningham said. He deftly threw down his crutch on his right side, pulled out his pistol from the holster under the left side of his jacket, and planted one round in Dr. Mansell's chest at point blank range. The bang made everybody but Mr. Rader flinch and a stony silence filled the room as Dr. Mansell immediately lurched over and fell face first onto the floor. Mr. Cunningham kept his pistol aimed at Dr. Mansell's motionless body for a few more seconds.

Lonnie gasped and started to cry, while everybody but Mr. Rader breathed a sigh of relief. Mr. Cunningham calmly put his pistol back in his holster and reached for his other crutch again.

"Crazy codger," he muttered to himself. "Now if you'll excuse me, I-"

Dr. Mansell's right hand sprang up and grabbed Mr. Cunningham's good ankle. The shock caused even Mr. Rader to shout from being startled.

"*HELP ME*!!!" Mr. Cunningham shrieked, as Dr. Mansell jumped to his feet and lifted his flailing body above his head. The pure white flesh, surrounding the bullet wound bubbled and pulsed, until it was healed in seconds, and left only an off-white, golf ball size scab. He hurled Mr. Cunningham across the laboratory like a rag doll. Upside down, the upper half of Mr. Cunningham's body hit the operating table in flight, which caused him to flip over the table, and crumple in agony on the other side.

"*RUN*!" Mr. Rader ordered the others and bolted out the main doors. The rest scrambled out with him, but Lonnie caught a final glimpse of her father. He picked up one of Mr. Cunningham's crutches and cornered him and Dr. Mansell's two masked medical assistants, just as Jerry slammed the main doors shut.

"*HELP*!!!" They could hear Mr. Cunningham's muffled last scream through the doors, followed by a series of thuds that grew duller as each thud passed.

"Oh God! Oh God!" Jerry shouted and began to hyperventilate.

"Brace the door!" Ali ordered.

Jerry and Vince frantically picked up a couple of chairs in the hall, dragged them over to the doors, and braced them under the handles. Ferris and Ali joined them in holding down the barricade. They had only second to catch their breath before they noticed that Mr. Rader and Lonnie had already ran away down the hall. They recoiled from the door hearing the sounds of shouting and gunfire through the door. One by one, the shots and voices grew fewer over the grunts, screams, crashes, and thuds until there was no more.

"C'mon! Move! That wasn't the only door out of the lab!" Lonnie shouted to Jerry, Vince, Ferris, and Ali.

"Security breach! Security breach!" Mr. Rader screamed at the end of one hall before he turned around to yell down the adjacent hall. "We have a hostile! Shoot to kill! Repeat! Shoot to ki-"

Lonnie had almost caught up to Mr. Rader when she froze in her tracks. Dr. Mansell pounced out from around a corner, tackled Mr. Rader and pinned him down to the floor. Lonnie screamed and ran back towards the others.

"Go! Go! Go!" she shouted as she ran and pointed ahead of her. "Back to the lab! Get those doors open!"

Ferris slipped a little as he turned tail to run, but Ali helped him up on his feet. By the time Lonnie got back to them, Vince and Jerry had yanked the chairs out from bracing the doors, and flung them open again. Down the hall, Mr. Rader wrestled Dr. Mansell on the ground and struggled to free his pistol out from his jacket holster. Dr. Mansell howled loudly and drooled all over him, until he finally got off a shot. It planted dead center of Dr. Mansell's abdomen, which allowed Mr. Rader just enough wiggle room to escape from under him.

He didn't have much time before Dr. Mansell staggered to his feet and started to pursue him again. Mr. Rader turned around to face him and walked steadily backwards and kept pace with Dr. Mansell's advance. He leveled his pistol off, held it tightly with both hands, and capped off the remainder of his clip. Each bullet, though skillfully placed, at one second intervals, on the head and chest, did little to slow Dr. Mansell down. Each wound bubbled over and scabbed just like the first one.

"Go!" Mr. Rader yelled to the others.

He quickly reloaded his pistol and turned to follow them into the laboratory when Dr. Mansell picked up his Ming vase in the hall, and hurled it at Mr. Rader. He managed to make it two steps before the large vase hit his back like a porcelain cannonball and shattered into a dozen pieces. Mr. Rader's broken body crumpled face down on the floor.

"Go!" he managed to let out to Jerry with a final, desperate wheeze, as blood began to trickle out of his mouth.

The others were already making their way out the lab's other exit. They hopped over the lifeless, mangled bodies of Mr. Cunningham and the medical assistants. Jerry saw Dr. Mansell grab Mr. Rader's ankle and drag his body backwards. As they ran out of the lab, they could hear Mr. Rader's final yell when he emptied his last clip into Dr. Mansell, and then there was silence.

Jerry was the last one out each door and frantically shut each one behind him, locked it, and dumped over random pieces of furniture, in an attempt to brace each door, while the others escaped ahead of him. But Dr. Mansell still gained on them. He could hear the grunting, heavy breathing, and the smashing of doors and furniture grow louder as they fled. Jerry suddenly stopped.

"Split up! Hide!" he shouted ahead at the others. "I'll draw him off!"

"No! Jerry! I really like you!" Lonnie screamed and turned back towards him.

Jerry made it a few steps away from the last door when Dr. Mansell already started to pound on it.

"Run! Now!" Jerry shouted, turned his back to the others, stepped away cautiously from the thumping door, and eyeballed the exit to his left. Vince grabbed Lonnie's shoulders and restrained her just as her father bursted through the last door and smashed it into splinters. Even though Jerry was over thirty feet away, he felt the air pressure changing as Dr. Mansell's breath had become gigantic in volume and even faster in rate. His gargantuan body was dotted from head to toe with cankerous bullet wound scabs.

"Daddy! No!" Lonnie screamed.

Her plea stunted Dr. Mansell's advance for a second, but he kept coming. Vince yanked her away and they ran. Ferris and Ali were already way ahead and out of sight. Jerry waved his hands as he fled to his left.

"Here! Here, Mongo!" Jerry screamed as he ran.

Dr. Mansell stomped towards him. His body had grown large enough now that it had to bend and burst through some of the mansion's narrow doorways.

Vince and Lonnie were just about to run outside, when Vince suddenly stopped in his tracks.

"C'mon! Let's go!" she demanded and tried to pull him away.

"I could really use a drink," Vince said plainly.

Lonnie stood dumbfounded.

Jerry ran for his life. Each yard, foot, and inch, he threw whatever he could at Dr. Mansell. Every step gained him just enough time to escape until he came to a room where the only way out was outside into the mansion's backyard. Without thinking, he burst into the backyard of the Mansell mansion and ran into the cool, night air. Dr. Mansell soon followed and shattered the flimsy wood and glass doors on his way out.

The last two security guards alive ran over from the mansion's parking lot to find them both.

"No! No! ***DON'T***!!!" Jerry screamed but it was too late.

The barrage of bullets only attracted Dr. Mansell to the last two guards, but it allowed Jerry to slip away. Blindly, he ran away from the mansion lit only by the moon toward the ocean. With the gunshots and screams at his back, he had nowhere left to turn. At last, he reached the property's end. The well-groomed lawn stopped and he found himself standing at the edge of a two hundred foot tall cliff. The brutal surf of the Pacific pounded away at the jagged rocks below him. Jerry turned back only to watch helplessly as Dr. Mansell's monstrous shadow drew closer. Jerry zigged and zagged for a moment in an attempt to get away, but the shadow would lurch toward either direction, which cut off any avenue of escape.

"Hey… Hey…" Jerry struggled to speak, but then sunk his shoulders. "Oh God… Oh God… No… No… No…"

Jerry turned to face the sea when he heard a voice from behind him.

"Hey, Doc!" Vince shouted. Dr. Mansell and Jerry both turned around to see that Vince was there and he held a lit, gallon size, Molotov cocktail in one hand and Lonnie by her arm with the other.

Dr. Mansell grunted angrily and took a step towards them.

"Here's to your health!" Vince shouted one more time and hurled the giant bottle at Dr. Mansell. The bottle instantly shattered dead center on Dr. Mansell's face and poured flaming liquid all over him.

Dr. Mansell's roar was deafening as he stumbled around, consumed by the flames. Instinctually, he ran towards the ocean, right in the path of Jerry. Lit only by the flames, Vince and Lonnie could see only blurs and shapes, as Dr. Mansell leapt off the cliff. Lonnie jerked away from Vince's grasp and ran toward the cliff, but saw no one. Vince joined her immediately, but also could see nothing but the pounding surf below.

"Uhh… A little help!" they heard just below them.

Their eyes adjusted to the dark and they spotted Jerry as he clung anxiously to the wet rocks just feet below them.

"Jerry!" Lonnie shouted over the noise of the waves and immediately stretched out her hand to grasp his. Vince joined her, grabbing his wrist, elbow, and shoulder, as Jerry made his way back up top. They all panted deeply while they tried to recover from the adrenaline rush, and hugged each other in the cool breeze. But then they heard a monstrous, gurgling groan from below them. They all sprang to their feet, but soon stood down, as they witnessed the fate of Dr. Mansell below them.

He struggled to cling to the giant, slick rocks, but the huge pounding surf kept beating his thrashing body against them. Lonnie buried her head into Jerry's chest, overcome from the horror of it. Jerry and Vince closed their eyes too. Only Lonnie looked down one more time to watch as her father was finally dragged into the deep by the riptides. Jerry and Vince opened their eyes and looked down the cliff.

"Is he gone?" Vince asked.

"I don't think I ever saw him swim," Lonnie said and wiped the tears from her cheeks. "But he did love living by the ocean."

"I'm so sorry," Jerry hugged her. "I shouldn't have let it go this far."

"No, I'm sorry," Lonnie replied. "I shouldn't have led you on."

"Hey!" a voice came from behind them.

They sprang into action, but relaxed when they saw Ferris and Ali as they emerged from the dark and joined them.

"I found a gun!" Ferris shouted and scanned his eyes around. "Where is he?"

Vince, Lonnie, and Jerry didn't respond. Instead, they just looked quietly over the cliff once more for a moment. Ferris finally got it, hushed up, and put the gun down.

"Are we it? Are we the only ones left?" Ali asked.

They all looked around and could hear nothing but the pounding surf.

"Guess so," Vince said and started walking back to the mansion. The others began to follow.

"We have to tell someone," Ali said.

"*NO!*" Jerry interjected. "You saw what happened! This can't become public."

"But what?-" Ali tried to speak.

"He's right," Vince said and his sarcasm leaked through his trauma. "This never happened. Hey, let's go back to the desert. After all, we have a photo shoot to do in the morning, right?"

"It's the only way!" Jerry insisted.

"How can we cover this up?!" Ali asked and pointed at the wreckage in the mansion as they approached it.

"Oh, I can take care of that. It's just…" Lonnie sniffled a little through her tears, but started to regain her composure. She stopped, took Jerry by the hand, and looked sweetly into his eyes. "There's a lot of bodies and I'm not that strong."

Vince, Ferris, and Ali looked at each other up and down. Entranced by a combination of physical exhaustion and love, Jerry smiled and nodded.

"If we haul ass, we could make it back by sunrise," Ferris said. "I know I'm not going to sleep tonight."

"Do you have a wheel barrow?" Jerry asked Lonnie.

"I could probably dig one up," she replied.

Chapter Sixteen

TEN YEARS LATER...

Jerry sat calmly in his new lab and stared through his microscope. A voice from the intercom on the wall startled him, which made him sit upright.

"Dr. Spencer, you have a call coming in," said the soothing female voice.

"Thanks, Fran," he said and glanced at the clock on the wall. "I'll take it at my desk."

He took a deep breath, looked back at his microscope for a moment, stood up from his stool, and walked over to a computer station across the lab. Jerry sat in the station's chair, punched up a few keys, and within seconds, Vince's smiling face was on the screen. Vince was calling from his smart phone and he wore a colorful tropical shirt. Behind him was a gorgeous white sand beach and orange sunset in the distance.

"Vince!" Jerry said.

"Hey bud," Vince said back.

"It's been… It's been…" Jerry trailed off.

"Yeah, way too long. Too long, for sure," Vince interjected. "Hey, it's my fault."

"No, no, no. It's mine," Jerry insisted. "You know with the company, the last product launch, Lonnie and the kids."

"Nah, it's me. The career, life on the island, Kate and the boys," Vince went on. "… And losing Dad."

"Yeah, I'm sorry as hell about that," Jerry said. "I should have come out to St. John's. It's just it happened so fast and-"

"Eh, forget about it," Vince reassured him. "You know Dad. Always wanted to keep a low profile."

"He was happy though," Jerry said.

"Oh yeah. I mean you remember what he was like before the…" Vince paused. "…well, before. These last years out here were easily his happiest."

They both took a moment to reflect, but before either could speak again, the lab's door opened and Dr. Jacobs walked in. He strutted confidently with a big grin and full head of white hair.

"Hey Jerry, you goin' with us to Happy Hour after-" Dr. Jacobs' attention was immediately drawn to Vince's face on the computer monitor. "Oh my God, Vince! Vince! It's you! I can't believe it! How are ya?"

"Hey, Dr. J." Vince waved at him through his phone. "Lookin' good, man!"

"Thanks!" Dr. Jacobs said and stroked his hair. "And thank Jerry here. If he hadn't gone back to redo the N series, we'd wouldn't have this little miracle. It's the real thing, baby! We made a fortune and put Rogaine and everybody else outta business! So what's up? When's the next album coming out?"

"Oh well, who knows?" Vince said casually. "Just enjoying my time now, looking after the family, sleeping in. I'll still do a couple charity gigs a month for the rich tourists just to stay in shape."

"Man, why don't you tour anymore?" Jerry asked. "You could fill stadiums all over the world if you wanted."

"You sound just like Dave, man," Vince joked. "You sure you don't want to get back into show biz?"

They were interrupted by a phone going off in Dr. Jacobs' pocket. He took it out and smiled even wider.

"Hey, that's my new girlfriend," he said and flexed both his eyebrows a couple times. "I gotta take this. You rule, Vince! Take care, man!"

"Yeah, you too, boss!" Vince said back.

"Hey, sweet thing!" Dr. Jacobs said into his phone as he left them room again.

"He looks great, doesn't he?" Jerry asked.

"It's amazing what a little formula can do," Vince sighed and paused a moment. "That's one of the reasons why I called."

"What's wrong?" Jerry asked immediately and grew concerned.

"Nothing, nothing wrong," Vince replied just as fast. "In fact, everything's as it should be. Let me show you something."

Jerry put on his eyeglasses and watched his monitor closely as Vince bowed his head. Jerry narrowed his eyes, watched Vince fiddle with the hair on the top of his head, and was astonished when he revealed a single strand of grey hair.

"Whoa," Jerry said under his breath.

"You see it, right?" Vince asked.

"Yeah," Jerry said, took off his glasses, and fumbled his words. "Yeah, I do. But... Uhh... How do you? ... When did this? ... "

"It's OK. It's OK," Vince reassured him. "I feel just fine."

"I could... I could run some tests... I-" Jerry said but Vince interrupted.

"No!" Vince lowered his voice. "No, no, no. There's no need. You saved me once already, remember? That's plenty."

"You sure?" Jerry asked.

"Sure I'm sure," Vince said calmly. "This is good news, Jerry. Good news. The formula brings you back, but it's not the fountain of youth. And that's a good thing. Besides, I wouldn't want to stick around in a world without Kate and the boys."

"Hmm." Jerry thought to himself for a moment. The pause was broken when Vince overheard somebody in the distance in front of him calling for him.

"Ooops! Well, that's my cue," Vince said and started to walk with his phone towards the bar of his beachside resort. "Time for another one of those charity gigs. I was actually supposed to be on stage five minutes ago."

"Thanks for calling, dude," Jerry said and grew sad.

"No worries," he replied. "Anytime you and the family want to come out, just let me know. First class all the way, my treat."

"Oh no, you don't," Jerry perked up. "I'm finally rich now, remember? I can afford it. Have a great show. Break a leg."

Vince stopped in his tracks for a second and they both paused, stared at each other for a second. They both remembered Mr. Cunningham and laughed out loud.

"Oooo-boy," Vince said between laughs.

"Poor choice of words." Jerry wiped away a tear and caught his breath.

"Be seein' ya," Vince said.

"Bye, Vince," Jerry said and they both hung up at the same time.

Back on the island, Vince held his smart phone in his hand for a couple more seconds and reflected pensively, until Kate walked up to him, flanked by two towheaded tan boys.

"Two gigs a month and you're still late?" she joked.

"Hey." He turned to face them. He hugged Kate first and then knelt to hug his sons. Kate smiled warmly, crossed her arms, but then appeared puzzled.

"You OK?" she asked.

"Yeah, yeah," he answered right away, let his boys go, and stood up again. "Everything's fine. C'mon."

His family followed him past the resort's bar. One by one, Vince passed the resort's patrons who cheered, patted him on the back, and shook his hand until he made it to the stage of the resort's outdoor auditorium. Vince caught a glimpse of Dave with his wife and her friends in the front row as they sipped their fruity cocktails. Dave put down his glass of orange juice, looked at Vince with playful disapproval, shook his head, and tapped the face of his wristwatch. Vince simply nodded and waved to the hundreds of cheering fans. He kissed Kate, grabbed a wireless handheld microphone, and strolled onto center stage.

"Hey folks!" he said to the crowd and squinted at the bright stage lights, took out a pair of sunglasses from his shirt pocket, and put them on. "Sorry I'm late! Glad y'all could make it!"

He turned around and faced his old band on stage, walked up to each of them, and shook their hands. Vince stopped at Ayman last, lowered his microphone, and spoke into Ayman's ear.

"You know, for a change I think I'll do the last one first, OK?" he asked him.

"Fine by me." Ayman smiled and mumbled to Kevin and Troy. They nodded back at him.

The crowd went wild as the band opened with the first few notes of "That's Life".

THE END

CPSIA information can be obtained at www.ICGtesting.com
Printed in the USA
LVOW130822220612

287149LV00006B/11/P

9 781432 793746